# DRAGON TWINS BRIDE

ALYSE ZAFTIG

EVA WILDER

# CONTENTS

# PART I

Phuong

*P*huong swallowed hard as she pushed open the door to the store. She hated doing this. Last time, her brother said. Just once more.

"Hello! How can I help you?"

She tried to ignore the sick feeling in the pit of her stomach as she smiled back at the store clerk.

Her eyes turned silver. "I need your help."

She could see the silver in her eyes reflected in the clerk's eyes.

"How can I help you?"

She couldn't control other people, but she could suggest things to them.

"I really need your help to get a key pass, but I don't have any money. Do you think that it would be fair to give me one, since I can't afford it?"

She nudged him in the right direction, but the clerk was the person who made the final call.

"I think that would be fair. What color do you want? Do you have a code number for the lock that it should open?"

Phuong hadn't thought through what color the key pass should be.

"Gold, please. And the code number is 5894."

"Coming right up." The clerk went to the back, got a gold key pass, and swiped it to activate it.

"There you go. Thank you for your business!"

Phuong nodded. "Thank you!" She took the gold key pass from the clerk and tucked it safely in her pocket. The bells chimed as she walked out of the store.

That was the last time. Xuan had promised her that

she'd only need to do it once more, just to get all of their ducks in a row. After this, her brother said that they'd be on easy street.

She trusted her brother, but she thought that he might have over-promised.

She slipped into the shadows as she neared the service entrance of the aquarium. Inside, there were burnished bronze tunnels that made a lot of noise if she was careless enough to touch the walls. She walked quickly and carefully towards the den that she shared with her brother, trying to be as quiet as a ghost. To her relief, she finally got to the hatch door that would let her into their living space.

It hadn't been easy to find a place, not when they didn't have any real money. They were stowaways from Heritage House, the group home where they'd been raised. It's not easy finding a place to live when you're wanted. Even harder when you can't live in a place connected to the city's water supply.

When Phuong or her brother Xuan used "tap" water, they broke out in full-body hives. Either they had to take antihistamines on a daily basis, or they had to use clean water.

The aquarium was one of the few places in town that had ultra-purified water, so they had to stay near it.

Phuong was ashamed about it, but it also had a steady supply of fresh fish. They were careful not to take too many or too much, but they sometimes had no other choice. At the most desperate moments, fish could get them through.

"Xuan?"

Xuan didn't reply, so Phuong went past the circular front area of their home. It had a bunch of water pipes that brought them their supply. She looked around their small living space, but Xuan wasn't inside. He must have gone somewhere.

Phuong settled down on one of the boxes that they'd taken from the aquarium. She stared at the Kiyin stone sitting on the mantel of the generator vent.

The Kiyin stone was the only clue to who they were. There weren't any other indications of where they'd come from when they landed on the doorstep of the group home.

It shimmered, just a little bit. It was obviously powerful, but they didn't know what it did. When they'd left, Xuan had stolen it from its place of honor in the head office.

As hungry and desperately poor as they were, it would've made sense to sell it. But Phuong and Xuan weren't willing to part with it. They'd kept it close in their den, and Phuong could feel something awakening inside of her gut.

She just knew that it was the key to something big, something that would help them figure out where they came from.

As she thought about it, her mind slammed into a stone door. She gritted her teeth. The implant in her brain that neither her brother nor Phuong had been able to overcome threw up mental blocks whenever she thought about something that the group home had deemed "dangerous."

Growling, Phuong went to her medicine cabinet. They were next to one of the least-visited tanks, and she could see an eye next to her, then a fin in the dark water. The little Kneck loved to visit them, probably because they were something new and shiny to look at.

She went to get a glass to take her medications. She gulped the whole thing down. Just being out and about made her so thirsty, but there wasn't a lot of water that she could drink.

Then she heard the hatch door open.

Phuong

"Where have you been, Xuan?"

"Did you get it?" Xuan answered her question with another question, avoiding the discussion.

"I did." Phuong pulled the gold key pass out of her pocket.

"Look. I've got blueprints." He pulled a roll of paper out of his pocket and waved it around.

"Blueprints? Blueprints of what?"

"The tunnels under the Alrech Auction House."

Phuong took in a sharp breath. "You can't be

serious. Xuan, we steal to live. We don't take the treasure of the mega-wealthy."

"Everything there would help us, but I want something that's going to set us free. We'll never run out of money again. We can live the life we've always dreamed of. We can afford to pay healers to take out our implants."

"Xuan..."

"I know that you don't like stealing or nudging people to help us, but if we do this one last time, we can be safe and happy forever. Do you want to scrounge in the tanks for the rest of our lives?"

"No."

"I need to keep you safe. There are too many people who take notice of you. In the last year, you've...grown up."

Phuong blushed. What he was trying to say, in his brotherly way, was that she'd developed in the last year...developed in ways that caught a lot of glances from random strangers. She was getting to be too remarkable to be an effective thief. If she was ever caught, Xuan wouldn't be able to get her out.

"You're crazy to try to steal from Marc."

"I know. I know. His reputation..."

"Xuan, if we get caught by Marc, then it'll be worse than going to jail. At least in jail, we'd have a roof over our heads, food to eat, and a bed to sleep in. If we get caught, we'll probably be fish food."

"Phuong, we have to try. He has Illinium ore that is worth thousands upon thousands of credits in the black market. I won't even have to arrange for transport off-planet! All I need to do is get it out of the auction den. I know that we can do it. We can do anything."

"Xuan, he's a Drakan. He's a shifter, and he can smell everything. He's going to know that we've been there."

"Not necessarily." Xuan pulled out a small bottle. "Smell this."

Phuong took the little bottle from his hand and unscrewed the cap. She took a good whiff and gagged.

"What is that?" She wiped her watering eyes.

"It's the essence of peppermint."

"It's...strong."

"Strong enough to mask our scents, I think."

Xuan looked at Phuong.

"I know you don't like stuff like this, but I swear, we can do this and be done. We can figure out a way to stop the group home from getting us back until we turn 21."

"I...I don't want to go to the auction house, Xuan. I don't mind taking a fish here and there, but stealing from Marc is a whole other level."

"We have to. There's no other way."

Xuan pulled out a sheet of paper and began to scribble down notes in his shorthand. For their whole lives, they'd seen symbols in their sleep, symbols that weren't anything like the Drakans' writing system. Xuan could use it perfectly, but Phuong took extra time to decipher the symbols.

Since they'd left the group home, they'd seen it in a couple places. When Xuan had finally worked up the nerve to ask what it was, they'd been told that the symbols were chu nom, not widely used but sometimes used for decorations.

Neither Xuan nor Phuong knew why they dreamed about decorative characters, but it was part of their past...something about which they'd never been able to learn much. Maybe they never would.

At least when Xuan wrote in chu nom, nobody could figure out what was going on.

# BLOOD THIEF

## Olivier

*O*livier felt someone touch his arm. He turned just in time to see someone trying to jab a needle into him.

"Get away from me," he shouted, deliberately attracting attention in the crowded marketplace. He heard a snap as he broke the man's pinky finger.

The thief, wearing ragged clothes, dropped the needle and ran through the crowd, disappearing behind people.

Olivier began to push people aside as he pursued

his would-be attacker, only to be stopped by a hand on his wrist.

"You better be ready to lose that hand," he warned as he turned around. "How dare you lay a hand on a prince?"

"When you're a prince, too, somehow the royal status doesn't mean much," his twin said drily. "Give up. He didn't take any of your blood. Your eyes are still glowing around the edges."

"He tried to stab me with a needle," Olivier protested. "I need to bring him to justice."

"Leave the cafard in his filth."

Olivier glared at the crowd. Thanks to his twin's intervention, he couldn't even see the thief anymore.

But Gahariet was already pulling him in another direction. "Forget it. Let's just head back."

As they walked towards the cobble road, they heard a shout. They were near the archives when an old woman hobbled towards Olivier. He'd had enough of being touched today, so he quickly sidestepped so that Gahariet was closer.

But she went towards Olivier, stepping too close to him. "Your fate is on the way. She will come, but trouble follows her closely."

The hair on the back of Olivier's neck stood straight up. He rubbed the back of his neck.

"Mother, don't bother the princes." There was a young man who put his arm around the old woman's shoulders and brought her to a small stall that was near the archives. "I'm so sorry, Your Highnesses. My mother...sees things sometimes. She says that it's her obligation to tell the people that she sees...she's never seen Drakan royalty before. Please don't arrest her. She's old and sick."

"We're not monsters," Gahariet said in his smoothest voice. Olivier shook his head. Gahariet had always been able to talk his way out of any sticky situation. They were in a crowded marketplace. Yore everywhere had turned to look at them. Yes, they would be within their rights to harm her, but they'd pay for it. "We appreciate her warning."

With a nod, the man disappeared with his mother.

Olivier turned to Gahariet. "What is it with

everyone wanting to talk to me today? My fate is coming? But she's in trouble? That could be interesting."

"Did you notice that her eyes were silver?"

"Yeah, freaky, right? Is that common?"

"I don't think so. I've never seen it before."

"Let's go home."

"I'm more than ready to be inside, away from all these people, believe me."

The two of them headed home.

# DINNER

## Phuong

*P*huong's stomach growled loudly, stirring her out of her meditative trance. She could see her face in a shiny piece of metal on the wall. Her eyes were glowing silver...just a little bit.

She clenched her fist. She'd been right at the edge of seeing something in her mind's eye. She could get there if it weren't for her stupid implant. She just knew it.

But until they could afford the surgery to get their implants taken out safely, she was stuck with it. There wasn't any point in getting angry about it.

The only thing that she could do was work towards the money that they needed to get the surgery.

They weren't doing it through the government-funded channels; they weren't supposed to take the implants out, so they'd have to accept a black market surgeon. Anything could happen, but Xuan was desperate to get the implants out of their heads. She figured that she'd go along for the ride. She didn't have a better idea.

She could smell something. Their den was mostly one space, but their "rooms" were little alcoves on each side. They were a little too regular to be there by chance, but when Phuong had asked Xuan about it, he'd just shrugged. She'd let it drop.

Her sheets were pure silk, the kind that they definitely should've sold a long time ago. It was strange how her brother insisted on having the best things even when they couldn't afford much.

The silk sheets had been a gift from her brother. Well, a "gift." He'd given them to her when she'd gotten him into a Drakan boutique with a little suggestion.

She put on her slippers, which, thankfully, weren't absurdly luxurious for their circumstances.

She went out into the main area. On their "stove," such as it was, she could see some pots with steam coming out of them.

"What are you cooking?"

"Amila stalks and lagoon-fresh greens," Xuan said.

Phuong pressed her lips together. Those foods were way too expensive for people who couldn't actually afford to feed themselves regularly.

She folded her arms. She counted to five. She was still mad. She counted to twenty.

She couldn't stop herself from saying, "We can't afford this."

"Or the wine."

"Xuan!"

He gave a wide grin, the one that had gotten him out of sticky situations without any silver-eye mojo. Her brother was a charmer, no doubt about it. It worked on random strangers and it worked on his sister. She just shook her head.

"Come on. Live a little."

"You're so focused on today's pleasures that you don't see that we're not going to have enough food tomorrow! I feel horrible when we steal fish from the aquarium."

"We won't be doing that for long."

She shook her head. "We don't have that Illinium yet."

"We'll get it. I'm sure of it."

"If you quote that motivational speaker one more time..."

"You have to believe it to achieve it. Positive thinking works, Phuong. You just have to believe it."

Phuong knew better than to argue with someone who was delusional. She'd never win a fight with her brother. He didn't like to see reality, and it was hard to be the realist. She wished that she could get a good dose of his optimism, but she was depressingly pragmatic. She went to their constantly packed trunk to get out some dishes.

She went over to their water spout to rinse some of their dishes off.

One of the other escaped orphans from Heritage House had given the dishes to Phuong, and she treasured them. Gifts meant much more from people who had nothing.

Like so much that they owned, it should've been sold for money to buy food, but they kept it still.

It was a reminder that even when they'd had their backs to the wall, when they'd owned only the clothing on their backs, that kindness had meant everything to them. They'd had to move on — their friend wasn't in a position to help them indefinitely — but shelter for just a few nights had meant everything.

Phuong tried not to worry about the cost of the Amila stalks — easily a day's wage for the average hardworking member of the middle class. The wine... imported from off-planet, since they didn't have the right land or climate for growing grapes for wine...was also absurdly expensive. The fresh greens could be an absurdly expensive price or just swiped from a garden.

Xuan was incredibly short-sighted. What if he had been caught? She would've been left alone, trying to get him out of jail.

"Set the table, please."

She looked at the dishes in her hands.

"Why is there a candle on the table?"

"It's a vanilla-scented candle."

Xuan, as ever, dodged the real question.

"We can't live like this. You know that, right?"

"Wine?"

Xuan ignored reality. Phuong was their pessimist. He was the idea guy... some ideas were better than others.

She looked at the spread on the dinner table.

"Looks good," she said, her shoulders slumped. The money was already gone. She couldn't magically make it reappear.

They sat down at the table, and, though they were paupers, ate like kings.

# DRINK

## Gahariet

Gahariet and Olivier were sitting at a bar, but they were having a lot less fun than usual.

"I didn't bring you here to obsess about what the Yore seer told you. Seriously, just let it go. There are so many angles, and it's probably not a legitimate prophecy. We're out to have fun. So drink."

Gahariet nudged a beer towards Olivier.

"But what if it's real?"

"We've chased this around and around. Some of

the Yore like to tug our strings, because they still resent our invasion of their planet. They don't have much power, so they do what they can to mess with us."

"Not all of them."

"True, some of them are real seers. But ever since our mother died, you've been too superstitious. Even when the seer actually can see the future, it can be changed with your choices today. Stop worrying and just chill."

Olivier looked up and met Gahariet's eyes, one corner of his mouth creasing in a lopsided smile.

"When have I ever steered you wrong?"

Olivier was the more free-spirited, emotional one, while Gahariet was the steadier of the two, the boring one, the responsible one.

"Never," Olivier admitted.

"You don't have control over what your future brings, so let's just hang out. Let's go downstairs."

Olivier got to his feet. Gahariet followed him down a short flight of stairs to the secret lounge.

Normal people came to the bar and had a great time. Below the festivities, there was another level for the nobility and royalty.

Down there, the wine was free. It was cheap in comparison to the membership fee to be let into a place that most people didn't even know existed.

It could be called a gentlemen's club, Gahariet supposed, but the nobility who came weren't on their best behavior inside. They weren't gentlemen.

Olivier and Gahariet pushed their way through the crowd that had amassed next to one of the stages to go to a far corner, where there was a naked girl serving wine. Olivier and Gahariet grabbed a glass of wine each while they watched the show.

Gahariet watched the nobility around the stage. Their eyes were looking at the naked girls like they were a nice piece of steak, not like they were sentient beings. Gahariet didn't like it. The club was a place where they didn't have to play by the rules. Gahariet didn't want to stick around. He drained his glass.

"I want to go home."

"Home? But we just got here."

Gahariet sighed internally. He'd brought his brother here to watch the girls, it was true, and his brother wasn't worrying about the prophecy anymore.

"We'll stay for a few more drinks."

Olivier nodded and got to his feet to get even closer to the stage. There was a woman on her hands and knees crawling near the edge. Anonymous male hands were tucking dollar bills into the straps of her shoes, because she wasn't wearing anything else..

Gahariet felt a flood of liquid hit him, getting his pants soaking wet.

"I'm so sorry," one of the naked girls gasped. "I didn't mean to spill wine all over you."

She had a glass of wine in her hand. Gahariet looked down at himself. It was red wine. The clothes were a total loss.

"I guess I should go home."

Gahariet was actually glad that he had a legitimate

reason to get out of this den of sin. He'd loved it when he was young, but he was just a little more mature now. He wanted more, a lot more.

Maybe it was because he didn't live in the moment quite as much as his brother, but he wanted to get started on putting together a family and producing heirs for the throne. He knew his duty.

Sure, he had a pretty enough face, and there were plenty of Draka nobles who would love to be princesses. But he'd met all of them and grown up with every one; he knew that he could never marry any of them.

He knew, that when he got old, they'd have to send to their home world for a girl who was fertile. He'd never find the right woman here.

"We have a clothes dryer in the back, if you'd like to come with me."

In a flash of light, Gahariet understood why she'd spilled wine on him. She wanted to get him naked. There were back room services that paid a lot more than working on the club's stage.

"No, thanks. I'll just go home."

He walked past her to get his twin, who was enjoying himself right by the stage...a little too much.

He yanked Olivier's collar.

"Come on. We're going home."

"But I was just..." Olivier's eyes went to Gahariet's pants.

"What happened to you?"

"Wine spill."

"Too far gone, brother? Can't hold your liquor?"

Gahariet slapped Olivier's arm. "Girl."

"Fine."

Olivier shook Gahariet off before making his way to the club's exit.

Gahariet was glad to go back to an area where the women were clothed. He hoped that the Yore women in that club were very well compensated.

They got into their private levi-car, which was in the valet parking area, before they came home. Gahariet was careful to sit on the edge of the seat.

They were more than wealthy enough to have two levi-cars, but their father was tight with his money. There was only one for the two of them, and Gahariet didn't want to get red wine on the seats. They'd be able to get it out of course, but they wouldn't be able to escape their father's lecture about wastefulness.

Gahariet sighed. Olivier's body was loose and relaxed. His head was back and he looked about twenty seconds away from sleep.

Gahariet, on the other hand, was wide awake. Funny how chilled wine in your pants kept you alert.

Soon, their levi-car was taking them to their door. It came to a stop outside of their home. Gahariet shook Olivier's shoulder. Olivier woke up enough to shuffle from the levi-car. He wasn't too steady on his feet. Gahariet realized that Olivier must've had more to drink in the brief time that they'd been apart.

"How much did you have?"

"Couple body shots," Olivier slurred. "Pretty girl."

Gahariet just shook his head. "You're going to have a killer hangover tomorrow."

"Be fine," Olivier protested. "Gotta live."

"Let me get you back into your suite."

Gahariet put his hand on Olivier's upper arm and guided him into his own room, where he flopped on the bed.

Gahariet touched the glow pad to turn off Olivier's lights. The rest was up to him.

Gahariet went into his own room.

As hard as he had worked to convince Olivier that the prophecy was a stupid sham, it was definitely possible that something was coming. Something big. Something that they didn't understand.

Gahariet didn't like not knowing what was happening. But he'd drunk just enough alcohol to make his eyelids heavy, so he fell asleep in his bed, still dressed in his damp pants.

# PERFECT DRESS

## Phuong

*P*huong was sweating, but it wasn't because of the heat. She'd lived here her entire life. The Draka were cold-blooded, and they could only survive in warm climates or ones that were artificially kept warm.

The Insa coins in her pocket were heavy. Xuan wanted her to buy the perfect dress, but she felt like she had a spotlight on her as she walked through the Draka boutique row.

There were immaculately beautiful and very wealthy ladies walking around with their friends.

Phuong stood out because she was walking around

solo. Her clothes didn't cost what a middle-class family paid for food for a year.

The Draka were all about deeply individual clothing; Phuong had mass-produced beige clothing that was made for the Yore. Anyone could see at a glance who was part of the upper class and who was part of the working class.

She'd never been in this part of the city. It wasn't meant for people like her. The Draka nobility shopped here.

Outside of the city, the wilderness with unseen wild beasts went right to the city walls. And while she wasn't keen on meeting any of the wild beasts that she could hear calling at night, she'd rather take her chances out there than right here in the heart of the Draka section.

Phuong wiped her forehead and tried to ignore the people staring at her. She walked as quickly as she could as she made her way into Dalshan's Dressing Hall.

The sound of the bells chiming when she opened the door startled her, making her widen her eyes. But she kept her chin up, as if she belonged here.

Like her brother said, you have to believe it to achieve it.

A store clerk came up to her.

"Can I help you?" The store clerk was a stunning Yore girl with waist-length hair and huge eyes.

Phuong watched her sweep her eyes up and down Phuong, as if she were something a little strange.

But the moment passed. "How can I help you?" she repeated, smiling kindly at Phuong.

Phuong knew that this shop assistant couldn't possibly be used to Yore coming in, but there was a moment of solidarity — two Yore women in a Draka-dominated world.

"I need a dress," she said. "A nice dress?"

The shop assistant, who was wearing a name tag that said that her name was Trang, brought her to another section of the store.

"We keep some dresses from last season back here. It might be better for your budget."

"No," Phuong said immediately. "I need the perfect dress." Phuong dug into her pocket for her money. She showed a fistful of the Insa coins to the store clerk.

Trang's jaw dropped when she saw the shiny coins.

"What's your upper budget?"

"I'll know which dress I want when I see it."

Trang took her to the front of the store.

"All of our newer dresses are up front."

Trang took several dresses off the rack.

The first one was a very bright orange with extremely deep cleavage and huge pockets at the hips.

"I don't think that would be very flattering."

The next one was a black dress with turquoise and purple flowers all over it.

"This one looks like it would fit you."

Phuong felt very self-conscious about her curves. Even though they scrabbled for food, somehow her body was still pretty curvaceous. Besides, she wasn't sure about mixing turquoise and purple.

"I think that this dress is pretty, but I'm looking for something spectacular. Something that'll make me a knockout."

"How about this one?"

Trang had pulled off a dress with lightly glowing mauve, indigo, and light pink flowers all over the top with a simple black skirt. The flower petals glowed gently under the filmy over gown.

"It's wonderful," Phuong breathed softly.

"Let's have you try it on, shall we?"

It was a wrap dress, so Phuong pulled the sash through the hole and then tied the whole thing together.

"Come out and show me," Trang called.

Phuong made a face at herself in the mirror before coming out.

"I think that it shows too much cleavage."

"No, I think that's the perfect amount. You wanted to be a knockout, right? Turn towards this mirror." Trang was pointing at a three-part mirror.

"I already..." Phuong was speechless when she looked at herself from three angles.

"Oh wow."

"Yeah. This dress looks like it was made for you."

Somehow, the dress was alluring without being overly revealing. Yes, you could clearly see the shadow between her breasts, but every bit of the solid under gown covered her up.

"I'll take it," Phuong decided. "How much?"

Trang named a price that made Phuong wince. This job better be worth it.

Phuong shelled out the Insa coins, and Trang took out a dress.

"I can wrap it in tissue paper for you."

"No, I want to wear it out of the store."

"That's fine. I'll give you a bag for the clothes that you're wearing right now." Without being told, Trang must have understood how much Phuong felt like a fish out of water.

Phuong went back into the dressing room to get her

clothes. Trang was waiting outside with the bag, where Phuong put all of her clothes.

"Thank you very much for your help," Phuong told Trang. "I appreciate it."

"Anytime," Trang said warmly. "I hope this dress works for you."

Phuong's eyes glowed silver as Phuong nudged her into forgetting what had happened. At least she'd had the money to pay this time. Trang's eyes echoed the silver in Phuong's eyes before she turned away as if Phuong wasn't even there.

The bells chimed as Phuong pushed open the door and stepped out into the sunshine.

This time, nobody gave her a second glance. There were plenty of beautiful Yore wives of Draka men, and dressed in her new clothes, she looked just like one.

Phuong walked back towards the aquarium, determined to do the best that she could.

When she got there, her brother opened the hatch of their den.

He let out a low whistle.

"Good job, Phuong. I think that this'll knock them dead."

"I hope so." Phuong touched the soft fabric of the black skirt. "I mesmerized the store clerk into forgetting me."

"Good. Soon, we're going to have so many credits that this dress will look like it was purchased second hand. You look beautiful, by the way."

Xuan didn't compliment her very much, and Phuong tried not to cry. There weren't very many moments of joy in their lives, not when they were poor and on the run. Xuan tried to fix it by spending money they couldn't afford to, and for once, he'd done something for Phuong that made her feel happy.

"I know. I don't feel like a cafard in this dress." The upper classes called the lower classes, the common Yore, roaches. It was so ingrained in the culture that even the Yore used it to refer to themselves. "I don't think that they'll treat me like I'm the low-born Yore that I am."

"We might be low-born, but we're not roaches. It's not our place."

"We can't be sure that we're low-born, honestly. We have no idea where we came from."

"Well, once we have the money for our surgeries, everything will be clear. Just one more job, and everything will be fine."

# RUN

## Olivier

"*I*'m going to go insane if I read another form or voting scroll." Olivier rubbed his eyes. He was tired.

Gahariet leaned back in his chair and looked right at Olivier.

"We can finish up for the day."

"I need to run."

"I'm starving."

"Let's grab something from the kitchen."

They closed their desks and headed towards the

kitchen, which was the hub of activity in their home.

There was a roast pig that was cooling on a rack. There were so many people in the kitchen that they were seen but ignored. Feeding all of them was a full-time task for quite a few people.

Olivier pulled a knife out of a chopping block and began cutting chunks of the roast pig and tossing them into a wooden bowl.

The two of them snuck out of the kitchen and ate the chunks of pork with their fingers, getting grease all over themselves.

Gahariet, ever responsible, made sure that the wooden bowl made its way back into the busy kitchen.

They washed their hands in a sink before disappearing. Their father made dinner served buffet-style, and people came in and out as they liked. They wouldn't be missed.

They had clothing in the stable that they used when they went running. They took off their official uniforms, the ones that they wore to look like Draka princes.

Their running clothes were contraband, but it was a secret that their hostlers were happy to keep. The stable master was old, and he had been the one to teach the boys to ride when they were younger. Horses and dragons mixed very cautiously; it required quite a bit of sensitivity. Olivier had, of course, taken longer to ride than perfect Gahariet. He'd been really frustrated when the stable master had kept him only mucking out his horse's stall for months after Gahariet was allowed to ride his horse.

Both of them went to their steeds to comb them for just a little while before they went for a run solo. After sitting all day, they didn't want to ride; their horses were exercised daily, so they weren't worried about their horses getting weak and fat.

Olivier touched his flat stomach. Gahariet was better about going out for runs. If he wasn't careful, he'd get too heavy. They both ate like the dragons that they were, but he wouldn't be able to fly if he got too heavy.

"Do you want to go to the Dawn Tower?"

The terrain around it was rough, but it would be strenuous enough for their dragon spirits.

They began to run to the Dawn Tower, which was only a few miles away. Olivier felt the wind go through his hair, and he felt alive. Why didn't he run more often?

As he ran and ran with his brother keeping pace next to him, he was reminded of his very young childhood. Their mother always took them outdoors. Their father was always busy, but sometimes he played hooky and went on picnics with them, which were sometimes near the Dawn Tower.

One of Olivier's first memories was playing hide and seek with Gahariet and seeing his parents kissing while he was the hider and Gahariet was the seeker.

It had seemed really gross to him at the time, but now, as an adult, he could see that his mother had been the love of his father's life — she'd tempered his rough edges. Once she'd died, his father had gotten a lot stricter. A lot more rigid. His queen should be ruling now.

Olivier felt an ache in his chest. He rubbed it.

Gahariet watched him do it, and Olivier felt self-conscious. He dropped his hand.

"Do you want to go home now?"

Olivier could remember why he didn't run that often now.

"Yeah."

They did an easy jog away from the Dawn Tower and the past.

Olivier gritted his teeth as he ran. Grown men didn't cry. They didn't. And if he panted especially hard, maybe it was because he was out of shape. And he was sweating a lot, enough that the sweat was getting into his eyes. And he might be wiping them, just to get rid of the stinging. Men didn't cry.

Olivier gritted his teeth as Gahariet easily ran back to their home.

"I need a shower," Gahariet said. "I'll ask for our servants to pump the water up."

"Sound good," Olivier said in his low voice.

Gahariet waved his hand over a glow pad before speaking into it quickly.

Olivier and Gahariet made their way back up to their chambers. He could hear the water running, so he knew that the servants had listened to them.

"Why do we have old pipes when we could just install Drakan technology?"

"This castle is made out of pure stone from the time when the Yore were in charge. It can't be modernized. You know that."

"Still annoying to have manually pumped water up here," Olivier grumbled.

"You're in a bad mood. Do you want to go to Arekir's party?"

"No. I smell terrible."

"I mean later."

"Getting dressed up in fancy clothes just to mingle with the usual boring people? The same ones, since we're only supposed to associate with a certain class of Draka. I'll pass."

"Maybe there'll be something interesting this time." But there wasn't much hope in Gahariet's voice.

"What else is there to do?"

"Good point," Olivier conceded. "We'll go. I'll be out in an hour."

Olivier went into his room and got naked before getting into his tub and washing away the grime of the day.

The clothes make the man, his mother used to say. Wearing his princely clothing made him a prince. Wearing a stable hand's clothing made him just a humble stable hand.

He wondered what it would be like, to really be free like that. Gahariet was the older twin, but he couldn't just strike out on his own and do whatever he wanted.

But he was a prince, even if he wasn't first in line.

He went to put on his shiny party clothes. He knocked on Gahariet's door exactly an hour after they came back.

"You're on time," Gahariet noted.

"Yeah."

"You really aren't yourself today. Are you sure you want to go?"

Olivier shrugged. "There's not much else for me to do."

## EVENING IN THE GARDEN

Olivier

Oliver and Gahariet took their levi-car to the party.

Even before going inside, Olivier was bored. Same faces. Same people.

"I hope they have alcohol."

Gahariet didn't say anything. They both knew that they had to put on public appearances, but it didn't mean that they'd enjoy them.

"Just the men I wanted to see!"

Olivier winced as he turned to the left to see an extremely large ball-shaped man coming at full speed towards him. He felt like a standing pin in front of an oncoming sports ball.

"Olivier! Gahariet!" The man hugged both of them in turn. Olivier couldn't even remember his name. Didier, maybe?

"I have the best news!"

"Oh?" Gahariet, who was far more polite than Olivier would ever be, raised one eyebrow, his tone cool and formal in contrast to the overly familiar hug.

"I have one of the best investment opportunities available. Just a little bit of a cash infusion and we could print our own money."

"We can already print our own money." Their father had plenary power, including the ability to make currency.

"Ah...yes...but I'm talking about business."

Olivier was already bored, but Gahariet was accepting two glasses of wine from a pretty Yore waitress dressed in a very low cut red dress. Apparently he wanted them to hang around.

"There's going to be an amazing auction tonight."

"Mhm," Olivier murmured, wishing that he could just go home. It was funny, because he was the more extroverted twin, but he didn't want to be here in a crowd of too-familiar people.

"There are going to be some very rare items there tonight. Some very rare items that might open up good doors."

Olivier stopped listening and scoped out the rest of the party. Gahariet always made sure that everything was on an even keel; he'd take care of it.

There were a lot more girls than there normally were at parties like this. It felt like he was surrounded by big, ostentatious flowers. The girls were dressed in vibrant colors, and a lot of the bolder ones made eye contact with him.

He felt like a fish in a room full of cats. His dragon spirit came roaring to life. A dragon was never prey.

He needed to get out of here.

"Sorry," he said, without a hint of contrition. "I just remembered that we need to be somewhere else."

"Somewhere else? But you haven't even heard about the..."

"No time," Olivier cut in.

"But I'll see you at the auction house?"

"Maybe." Olivier tugged Gahariet's hand. Gahariet, always polite, gave a simple nod to their companion before they went off.

"Where are we going?"

"Tally boards."

"Again? I thought you stopped betting after you lost a month's allowance in ten minutes."

"We don't have anything better to do. Besides, I like to watch the fights."

"They're underground fights. If you get caught... what would our father do to you?"

"Don't know. Don't care," Olivier said cheerfully. "He stays out of our lives, and we stay out of his."

"If there isn't anything interesting when we go to the tally boards — should we really be in that part of town? — then we're going home."

"Yup. I can promise you that much."

PREP TIME

Phuong

huong used a damp bit of cotton in order to fix the wing of her eyeliner. The bit of her skin that was touched seemed to shine, but it was probably just the water.

Phuong looked at herself in the mirror. On another day, she would've thrown a fit about just how much money they'd had to spend on the makeup kit, but it was necessary. She needed to fit in at the auction house. She couldn't afford the tiniest slip that would get them caught.

Oh, she could mesmerize a single person, sure, no

problem. But she couldn't do a crowd, particularly not with her implant.

She didn't know what she could do, since she couldn't remember a time that she didn't have it. But she had a feeling that she could blast a larger number of people if only she didn't have the implant.

She heard the thunk of a drawer closing behind her. Xuan was dressed to the nines.

"Are you ready? Hurry up!"

Phuong used makeup fixing spray to make sure that everything stayed where it was supposed to be. She picked up another canister of hairspray to make sure that her hair stayed in its elaborate hairdo.

The silvery spirals of her hair were adorned with stop-motion blooming and budding flowers in all the colors of the rainbow. They were kept in place with pins. She'd undergone a lifetime of torture at the hands of a hairdresser that afternoon.

This job better be worth it. Phuong wasn't into girly-girl stuff, partially because she'd never had the money and partially because it was just impractical.

"Done."

Xuan opened the hatch of their den.

"The future is ours to write. Come on! Time to ride the affirmation train."

"Tonight will change our lives for the better."

Phuong looked at herself in the mirror, so dressed up that she was basically a stranger. She didn't know the person in the mirror, but that person was about to steal from one of the most dangerous Draka in the city.

## TEA LEAVES

### Hoa

*N*o matter how many times she brewed the tea leaves, they always told her the same thing.

The time of the Yore resurgence had come, but it was a crossroads. The Yore would inevitably rise, and she knew that it's what they'd hoped for since the day that the Draka had taken over the planet.

But there was a shadow over their savior. She could land in the wrong house. If the savior's powers were turned in the wrong direction, it could corrupt the Yore resurgence. Even as they rose from under the Drakan heel, they would rebuild in a way that would fall apart.

"Mother, you shouldn't have run out to the princes."

"Child, it's my sacred duty to…"

"Not get killed." Vien put down his satchel on the table. "You could've been arrested if the princes wanted you to die in a prison."

"There are worse things." She loved her son, but he didn't have the Sight. He didn't understand the compulsion to warn people of their futures.

"There are dark circles underneath your eyes. You need to sleep more."

"I've seen the future."

"You have precognition. You always see the future."

"There's never been a more dangerous time."

"Especially for you, if you refuse to stay away from Drakan royalty."

"What are you talking about?" Hoa's brother, Trai,

came in. "Can you see the Drakan royals' future? Anything that would help us slaughter them?"

"Nothing. I didn't see anything." Her brothers hated the Drakan boot more than anyone else. If they'd seen the princes alone in the market, they would've attacked, no matter what the consequences were. They could just about stomach trading with Drakan merchants for necessaries, but they hated the royals, who symbolized all the brutality that the Drakans had brought to the planet.

A piercing baby's cry interrupted them.

"I need to check on her." Hoa walked out, away from her brother and her son. His daughter, her granddaughter, had just woken up from her nap.

"It's okay," Hoa cooed to the tiny baby who was doing her best to get as much attention as she could. "It's okay." She picked the baby up out of her cradle and held her. The baby stopped crying.

The baby's whole body was shaking with hiccups from the ferocity of her crying.

Hoa walked in a slow circle around the baby's

room. She pulled from the wellspring of peace in the center of her chest to chant the song of Aloka, the Yore queen who had ruled the Yore for two decades. After she died, she became a spirit of health and hope.

Even now, there were Yore priestesses who made regular offerings to her spirit. Most Yore only knew her song, used as a lullaby.

It could give hope in the darkest circumstances. The song could fill their hearts with light when they were near being overcome with despair. It was the last strength of the Yore.

The baby let out a little chirp.

"Hungry, baby?" Hoa walked the baby into their small kitchen, reaching for a bottle. Her daughter-in-law would love to feed the baby herself, but she was still working.

She got a pillow and fed the baby carefully. Her granddaughter had eyelashes long enough to rest on her cheeks.

When the bottle was done, her eyes had drifted all the way shut. Even though she'd just woken up, she was ready to be put down for another nap. She was still at the age when she slept constantly.

She put the baby back into her room. She realized abruptly that her son and brother had vanished. Where could they have gone?

She looked down at her darling granddaughter. She hoped that by the time she was an adult, the Yore would be free again. It was a possible future.

## TALLY BOARDS

Gahariet

"You're crazy. He'll never make it." The two of them walked away from the tally boards.

"He's got a crazy uppercut and he's great in a pinch. So what if he's a little short? He's got so much power. He's so good in the ring. People barely touch him."

"You just want to cheer for the underdog."

"Guilty."

Olivier nearly slammed into a man. Gahariet put a hand on his brother's arm.

Olivier let out a little bit of flame.

"Watch where you're going," he snapped at the man, who had the wall.

Olivier's body language dramatically changed when they saw who it was.

"Hello, Marc."

The owner of the Alrech Auction House was rubbing his hands together, the events of just seconds before forgotten when he looked at good prospects.

"Looking for a little excitement."

Before Gahariet could stop him, Olivier said, "Yes."

"What do you have?" Gahariet asked.

"I'm sure that tonight's auction will have something that will interest one or both of you. I can give you passes."

"We're princes. We don't need passes."

"Just complimentary passes, that's all."

Gahariet knew that Olivier was ready to start

flaming again. Gahariet tightened his grip on his twin's arm.

Marc looked from one brother to the other. Gahariet didn't like the grin that was spreading on Marc's face.

"I have to go on my way. I have a lot of things to do before tonight. I hope that you will be there. My seers have predicted an eventful night and unexpected treasure."

He nodded at the princes before going on his way. Gahariet and Olivier watched him go away.

"Why is everyone always overly familiar with us?"

"Our father is locked away with matters of state. We're the face of the royal family."

"I guess." Olivier sighed. "Do you want to go to the auction house? We could just go home."

"Why don't we try it out? It can't hurt."

"What is it with Marc's Yore seers? Are they real?"

Gahariet nodded. "Yeah. He searches for seers especially, and they're paid very well to stay with him. If you can predict the future of all of your business decisions, then…"

"You're always going to come out on top."

"Marc doesn't have a title, though."

"I didn't know that you were a snob."

"It was an observation, nothing more." Gahariet shrugged.

"I wouldn't be surprised if he married his way in. There are plenty of us who don't have any cash, despite having holdings."

"Not my problem. But why not check it out?"

"It might be fun. Why not?"

# PLUS ONE

## Phuong

*P*huong's heart was beating hard in her chest when she gave her forged pass to the attendant, a Draka man.

But he barely seemed to even notice Xuan, staring instead at Phuong. She guessed that she was disarmingly beautiful tonight.

The two of them went through the door and went into the very first room.

It was dedicated to antiques. Phuong gritted her teeth. It would take them longer to find the Illinium. It wouldn't be in one of the official rooms that were open to anybody walking through.

It would be in the underground storage part of the auction house, kept under lock and key until a buyer with ready cash was ready to claim it.

Phuong and Xuan had studied the blueprints until they knew them by heart. The access to the underground tunnels leading to the Illinium was in a secluded corner of the auction house. There was no sure way to penetrate the tunnels from outside of the auction house. If there had been, Phuong would've chosen that rather than entering the jaw of the dragon.

Xuan had done thorough reconnaissance. They would set off alarms if they tried to do anything else, so they were going to do this in the light.

The Draka were fiercely possessive of anything that they considered "theirs." Even things that weren't for sale were kept behind many doors that could only be accessed with the right passes.

The right kind of access passes had taken a month to acquire. Phuong felt them nestled next to her stomach in the bottom half of her dress.

She felt like the Drakan guards could see through her clothes straight to the contraband passes. She was sweating, and she was grateful that her makeup seemed to be holding up.

Xuan and Phuong drifted towards the secret door while appearing to peruse the auction items. The guards kept their eyes on them. With their slightly darker skin, they stuck out in a room of Drakans. There had been enough intermarriage between Yore and Drakans that they could be Drakan nobility, but they didn't carry themselves with the same kind of pure confidence that was bred in the bone.

Right on time, a bit of smoke wafted through the ventilation. Phuong could see the guards' eyes widen as they quickly went to the source of the smoke, which was safely as far away as possible from the secret door while still being inside of the auction house.

Without any supervision, Phuong and Xuan walked towards the door, pulled out the pass, swiped their pass, and entered the protected halls of the auction house, the ones that would take them to the tunnels.

The secret door closed with a loud thunk. Xuan

thought that there were probably security cameras around here, but whoever was watching them wasn't part of the normal guard.

Phuong crept right along the wall. Xuan turned to give her a wink as they made their way even deeper in.

She pulled out a second pass, but there was a Draka guard.

"What are you two doing here? Nobody is supposed to be..."

Phuong gritted her teeth as her eyes turned silver.

"We belong here," she intoned. "You never saw us."

"You belong here," he repeated. "I've never seen you."

The moment passed as the guard moved along.

"You belong here," he repeated again.

Phuong told Xuan, "I hope that he's not stuck like that."

"It's fine. It'll wear off. Don't worry about it. Focus on the mission."

Phuong hated being a thief. Yes, they had the right talent for it, but she didn't like taking things that belonged to other people.

As they went through each door, they got closer to the Illinium. Phuong wondered how they were going to get out quickly, but she decided not to borrow trouble.

"Just one more door and we'll be in Marc's hoard."

Then they went through the door using the pass, and they were greeted with the sight of more treasure than they ever knew existed.

"What is all of this stuff?"

It looked like a crazy person's home. There were a lot of different things all over the place.

"Search for anything that might contain Illinium."

"How much time do we have?"

"Not very. About 10 minutes."

All that effort, over a month of working, just for 10 minutes inside of the hoard. Phuong really hoped that their mission was successful. It would stink if they'd worked so hard for nothing.

## GLITTERING HOARD

Phuong

*P*huong looked at the wealth in the auction's underground tunnels. How many families could it feed? Nobody on Vestra would ever need to go hungry again.

She tried to focus on the Illinium. They wouldn't have a buyer for anything else, but Xuan's contact was very interested in acquiring Illinium, and he had a good underground reputation among the Peddlers, a reputation good enough for Xuan to go on this incredibly risky mission.

They'd already used up at least 8 minutes of their time, if not more. Phuong wished that they had practiced this part beforehand. They hadn't found as much Illinium as they wanted, and surely the guards would've noticed that the dark-skinned duo was gone.

They also had to make it through all of the doors that they had passed through on the way in. Carrying the Illinium and running out would be harder.

There was a pouch for it under the skirt of Phuong's dress. She just hoped that they didn't ask her about her sudden pregnancy.

There would be no second chances. The effort involved in getting in was intense, and the whole auction house would be on high alert once they realized that they had been robbed.

"I've got enough," Xuan told her. "One minute to go. Let's get out of here."

The two of them hurried out. Xuan didn't even take the time to put the Illinium in its hiding place. Their first priority was getting out. Not that many people knew what Illinium looked like. They thought that it was just platinum.

They were nearly to the door when Phuong tripped over an object, which would have been a big deal, except she fell to the side.

All of a sudden, the floor gave way. She held back a scream as she fell downwards at least 20 feet.

"Phuong!" Xuan looked around. "We don't have time for this. Grab my hand."

Phuong shook her head. "Xuan, get out of here and take the Illinium with you."

Xuan put the Illinium down and reached down as far as he could to no avail.

Their mission had failed. Yes, they'd gotten Illinium, but they wouldn't make it out of here.

Phuong looked around her, but the pit didn't have any way to climb out. Her eyes stung as she acknowledged the truth: she was truly caught. Xuan already knew it.

"You need to get out of here right now, before someone comes."

"I'm not abandoning you."

"Don't be stubborn and get caught."

"I'm not going to leave you here."

"They'll be nicer to me than they would be to you. Get out of here. Sell the Illinium. When I can, I'll come back to our home."

They could both hear the echoes of footsteps and the murmur of voices.

"Go!"

"I can't."

"I will never forgive you if you don't save yourself now. You know that the penalty for theft is hard labor for the rest of your life. I won't tell anybody about us. I'll say that this was my job, solo. You need to go."

Xuan hesitated only a second more before darting off the way that they came.

# RACING SMOKE

### Olivier

"**A**re you sure that we should go?" Olivier turned to Gahariet as they exited their levi-car.

"We might as well. It's better for us to keep an unofficial eye on Marc than to be left in the dark."

"He's one of the Fontaines, right?"

"Yeah."

"Keep your friends close."

"Your enemies closer. Yeah, I know. They could've fleeced our great-grandfather out of his throne."

"Why don't we fly?"

"Instead of taking the car?" Olivier shrugged. "It's easier to let something take care of everything. Our levi-car can navigate better than I can. I'm pretty bad with maps."

"Race you!"

Running to some open space, Gahariet shifted into his dragon form.

"Cheater!" Olivier shouted at his twin before he shifted, too. He followed his twin straight to the auction house.

The twins were nearly identical in their dragon form, but Olivier had amber eyes while his twin had green ones.

They raced quickly through the air, twining around each other and nudging each other as if they were children.

They got to the auction house swiftly. With twin thuds, the dragons landed on the rooftop of the auction house. They switched back to human form, the wind rustling their hair.

Gahariet ran a hand through his hair. "Let's go down."

They found a door in the roof and went down.

Immediately, they were stopped by an armed guard.

"Who are you?"

"Princes Olivier and Gahariet," Olivier snapped back. "Marc invited us himself."

The guard grunted as he pulled something up on his holo-screen.

"You're clear." The guard got out of the way.

"Honestly," Olivier said to Gahariet.

"He's just doing his job."

"I hope this auction is worth the trip."

"I think that Marc was just pulling our strings."

"Maybe, but it's unlikely that the Yore seers would lie to him about what's happening tonight. It could get interesting."

As they got into the main room, a very beautiful

young Draka girl dressed in a periwinkle gown with transparent sleeves and a deep V-neck came up to them, a tablet in one hand.

"Hello. I'm Lana. Such a pleasure to meet you two, Your Highnesses. Is there anything that I can do for you two?"

"Just get us a couple drinks and we'll be fine," Olivier said. She was a lot nicer than auction employees had been to them before. Still, they'd need the alcohol to handle Marc, even if his brood was suddenly kinder to them tonight. Marc always wanted to be the best, which was hard to do if you were competing with princes.

But Gahariet and Olivier made their way around the first room, noticing that not many people were all that interested in antiques.

Where was their host? After a half hour, Olivier knew that something was strange.

The cheaper items were on display now, but the more expensive items were always auctioned by Marc himself. He also always showed his gallery of display pieces, just to rub it in the noses of his clientele that he had possessions that they couldn't buy.

It was always a good show.

## CAPTURED

### Phuong

*P*huong tried to figure out how to hide under the mountain of pink minerals that lined the pit.

She heard the door open and she knew that Xuan was safe.

Her gut twisted as she thought about what would happen to her. She'd known that something would go wrong, but Xuan was always going on about positive affirmations. She wanted to support and believe in him. She didn't know that she'd be trapped in the auction house.

She heard footsteps getting closer and closer to the pit. Then she saw a face peer inside.

Her heart sank. The Drakan's face was curious. She held her breath as they made eye contact.

"I'd wondered where you'd gone. Going into an auction house that you're planning to steal from and attracting every eye in the room is a stupid plan."

He smiled at her. She didn't like it at all.

"What's your name?"

"Phuong."

Marc shook his head. "We'll have to do better than that."

Phuong didn't like the look in his eyes at all.

"It was foolish for the two of you to come here. But I will accept you in exchange for whatever your brother stole. I'll get someone to help you out."

He walked away. Phuong hugged herself down in the pit.

Soon, there was a metal basket lowered into the pit.

She stepped inside and was lifted high. When she got to the ground level, she tried to get out, but the basket's metal rods were extended.

"Hey!" she said.

"You need to be in your display case. Showtime is too soon."

Display case? Phuong didn't like the sound of that.

"Who are you?" The operator of the lift wasn't Marc.

"My name isn't important."

"Where's Marc?"

"None of your business. I need to hurry if you're going to be displayed on time."

Phuong screamed as her cage was swung into a slot in the treasure room, a wall of sections that were like a honeycomb, each section a separate, smaller room within the large one.

She found herself in a smaller room with an elderly Draka woman.

"Yore girls are so plump," she said disapprovingly.

"Don't you ever think of cutting back on your food?"

Phuong bit back a retort. Food had been in scarce supply lately, and she still looked curvy.

The woman sighed. "I might be able to find something that might fit you. Something stretchy or maybe a wrap dress. Wait."

Since Phuong was literally in a cage, she couldn't really do much else.

"Wrap dress, I think. Let's get...that...off of you."

Phuong looked at her dress. She hadn't noticed before, but her fall had ripped the bodice of her gown. Things were popping out, giving Marc and the lift operator a free show.

Phuong's cheeks turned pure red. She pulled together the pieces of her expensive but ruined dress with one hand, but the damage had been done.

"Off," the woman said impatiently. "Are you slow?"

Phuong pulled her ruined dress off. The woman

thrust a floor-length scarlet dress through the bars of Phuong's cage.

"Hurry up. You have to be ready in time."

Phuong looked at the red gown and thought about refusing.

"Don't even try," the woman warned. She crossed to the side and took a wand.

"Do you know what this is?"

"No."

"It can send different voltages through you at a distance. If you would like to be shocked into behaving, I'm more than happy to do it. You Yore don't know how to act."

"I don't need a cattle prod. I'm not a cow!"

"Then don't behave like one."

She looked at the red gown again. In other circumstances, she'd be happy to wear something so beautiful. It was a princess's dress, and she was just an orphan. How could something that looked so innocuous be part of something bad?

Now she was a doll, a possession. She would wear what they wanted her to wear.

She didn't know if they would report her, but the Draka justice system didn't have a lot of mercy for Yore renegades. Even something as simple as stealing was punishable by death. There were far fewer Draka than Yore. The Draka maintained their stranglehold on the planet by being as brutal as they could be. If any Yore put a toe out of line, her life would be forfeit. Any of the Draka could make the call.

She felt sick to her stomach. She'd gone here for their very last job, and now she would be trapped for only stars knew how long.

She didn't like being caged or displayed, but she put the red dress on anyway. The bodice seemed simple enough when she'd first gotten it, but it showed far too much of the shadow between her breasts for her comfort. What were they going to do to her?

"What is that unsightly bump at the base of your skull?" the woman asked.

"It's my implant."

"That will definitely be removed today. Now. I don't want any buyers to think that you're defective."

Phuong's heart soared. Could she get the implant removed today, even without paying an exorbitant amount to a black market surgeon?

The woman went to a glow pad on the door. Phuong's cage was pushed out into the main room and placed into a small room that smelled like antiseptic.

"Hello," a man wearing a healer's white robes said to her, ignoring the fact that she was caged.

"I hear you have an implant that I should remove."

"Yes," Phuong whispered, terrified that he would change his mind.

"I'm afraid I'll have to knock you out for its removal. General anesthesia for a little while."

With that, he slapped a button. A robot arm grasped a needle firmly. Before Phuong even had time to relax, the needle was jabbed into her.

Her eyes closed.

## COLLECTOR

## Marc

**M**arc adjusted his cuffs and checked every inch of himself in the mirror. He gave himself a disarming smile. If he charged premium prices, he needed to look the part. He smoothed his hair into place, making sure that there weren't any wayward strands.

He turned to his body servant.

"I want you to fetch my new prize."

"Which prize, sir?"

"The girl. Make sure they dose her before she's put on display. We wouldn't want her to cause any trouble. It's her first night here, so she doesn't understand how we do things."

"Very good, sir." His body servant went out the door.

Marc would display her alongside the other priceless objects that he only displayed with a simple NFS on the sign to tell people that they weren't for sale. A lot of objects passed through his hands, but this girl, Phuong, was something special. He'd have to think of a better name for her, a Draka one instead of her boring Yore one.

Something about her was so enticing...maybe entrancing was a better word.

On another night, he would've brought her to see his Yore seers so that they could sample her energy and find out more about her.

She was extraordinarily beautiful, with dark skin and pure silver hair. He'd never seen a woman like her. She looked like an angel, with perfect, full lips, which were two-toned.

If Marc had believed in a deity, then he would've thought that she was created by a loving one. She's the kind of woman a Drakan would love to fill with babies.

Fertile women were in short supply on the Draka home planet, and they'd found to their delight that Yore women had an easy time conceiving, which had resulted in quite a few Draka-Yore hybrids.

Marc left his room and went to the one-way glass pane that he kept so that he could survey his kingdom.

He snorted when he saw Olivier and Gahariet. The twin brats were in his auction house; they'd taken him up on his offer. They were wastrels, and their station was totally wasted on them.

Marc smiled slowly. He couldn't help but love the ability to strut a little in front of them. This auction house was his domain.

A never-ending thirst for treasure was in dragon blood, and Marc had built an empire by using that thirst. He'd started from nearly nothing. Giving people what they wanted was surprisingly hard, but that was why he was the best.

He straightened his collar and glanced one more time in the mirror.

Time to go downstairs.

# DISPLAYED

## Phuong

*P*huong's eyes were half open as the lush curtain was drawn back from the walls of her cage.

To onlookers, her cuff bracelets probably looked like elaborate jewelry. It would be hard for a casual observer to notice that her hands weren't simply folded in her lap; the cuffs kept her in that position.

The drugs had done the rest. That anesthesia had really done the trick, and she suspected that the doctor had overdosed her. She was fighting to open her eyes at all.

There was a fierce ache where her implant used to

be. It had been hidden in her hair for years; it was practically a part of her body.

She didn't want it, but her stomach turned when she thought about what the future might hold now that the implant removal had happened. She'd thought about it, of course, when they were making plans — but she didn't know if it would work.

She could already feel that she had access to a little more, but she didn't know what.

Marc's voice was loud and magnified. Whatever speakers they used were making her cage vibrate.

The onlookers walked away from her cage. Apparently a subdued and half-asleep Yore girl wasn't very interesting.

There was only one person left there. He was definitely a wealthy Draka.

Was he going to buy her? Phuong couldn't wipe away the tear that leaked from her eye with her hands bound.

"Did you choose to be auctioned?"

Phuong tried to open her mouth, but she couldn't

move her tongue properly. With a lot of effort, she closed it.

The Draka frowned. "Hm. You know what? I think that I can help." He winked at her.

He bit his lower lip deliberately, hard enough to draw blood. A few drops came out. He put his long, elegant index finger to his lip to catch a little blood.

Then his long arm was coming straight through the bars of Phuong's cage. His finger was making its way inside of her mouth.

The second that the blood touched her tongue, her tongue tingled. She reflexively sucked all the blood that she could from his finger.

Then she caught herself. What was she doing? She didn't know this guy. Who knew what else was on his hands? Had she really just drunk a few drops of his blood?

But the tingling was spreading throughout her body. First it went to her throat, but her body was thawing like ice in the springtime.

She flexed her hands in the cuffs.

She could talk now. "My hands are tied."

"I can get you out of this cage."

The Draka pulled a small gadget from an inner pocket.

"What's that?"

"Something that ensures that I'll never have to call a locksmith."

He put it against her cage's door. They both heard the click as the door unlocked.

And then he was leaning into the cage and putting it on her handcuffs. She was able to pull her wrists out of them.

He took her hand and brought her out of the cage.

"Olivier, what are you doing?"

"Gahariet, I thought that this lovely lady needed a little help."

"What have you done? You're so impulsive."

"I saw someone in need and helped them. Is there anything wrong with that?"

Gahariet just shook his head and opened his mouth. Instead of words, he expelled smoke which quickly settled into a simulacrum of Phuong, complete with the cuffs that were really on the floor of the cage.

"This could buy us some time." He closed the cage again. "They'll be able to see you inside of your cage, which is all that they'll need until the end of the night. We can maintain it for as long as you like."

"We need to get out of here," Olivier said. "I don't want to tangle with Marc, not on his own ground."

"Agreed," Gahariet said in his smoothest voice. "I know an exit."

Phuong did, too, but she'd memorized the blueprints before going on this job.

"How do you know an exit that wouldn't be guarded?"

The three of them were drifting towards the door.

"Our family used to own this building before it was sold and ended up as an auction house."

"Your family?"

"The royal family. The state, I guess."

Phuong stopped walking.

"What?"

"We're princes." Olivier cut straight to the chase.

Phuong's breath started coming in fast pants. Out of the frying pan and straight into the roaring fire.

She was sweating now. She really needed to get out of here and away from the Draka princes. She cursed her luck. Of all the people that could break her out of that cage, why did they have to be Draka princes?

"You don't need to take me. I can get out another way." Phuong turned away from them.

"You're safer with us." Olivier lightly touched Phuong's upper arm.

Phuong couldn't think of anything less true, but she tried not to hyperventilate.

"I'm fine. I can take care of myself."

"You ended up in a cage at an auction. Obviously, you can't."

Phuong's jaw dropped. She glared at Gahariet.

"Why do you even care?"

"Because you drank my blood," Olivier said.

"Yeah, when I was immobile."

Olivier had the grace to look ashamed.

"Yeah."

"What is in dragon blood?"

"That's a complicated question, but what's important for you right this moment is that we are blood bound."

Phuong was dumbstruck. Olivier put his arm around her and drew her with them as Gahariet brought them to the exit.

Then they were leaving the building. As they predicted, there weren't any guards there.

"What do you mean that I'm blood bound?" she asked, hurrying with them.

"We're blood bound. You drank my blood and bound yourself to me."

Phuong looked at the twins, one with amber eyes, the other with green. Phuong broke into a flat-out run.

But she'd only run a few hundred yards before smoke materialized in front of her and the twins were blocking her advance.

"Don't be afraid," Gahariet said soothingly. "We've waited a long time for someone like you."

# PART II

# WEAPONS ARCHIVE

## Gahariet

Gahariet opened the drink cabinet in their weapons archive. They had a real armory, of course, but the weapons archive was where they kept their family's old weapons. Their grandfather had believed that preserving the history that went along with their family was important, so he'd built a room to showcase all of the weapons that their family had used over the years on different planets.

Gahariet privately thought that their grandfather had built the weapons archive to get a bit of peace. Their grandparents had had a good relationship, but his grandmother got to be a little much sometimes. His grandfather had been very fierce, but he had loved them in his own way.

Gahariet offered a glass of red wine to his twin.

"Who thought that we would meet our mate in Alrech Auction House?" Olivier asked.

"Not me, that's for sure."

"You've smelled her?"

"She's definitely our mate," Gahariet confirmed. "Her smell...I feel like it's imbuing every part of me with her. I thought that you were reckless to break her out. It's not like we want to go toe to toe with Marc, not for a good reason at least."

"She's a good reason," Oliver protested. "Our mate is worth whatever trouble she brings."

Then Olivier blinked.

"The prophecy."

The edges of Gahariet's mouth turned down.

"She's our mate. We have a blood right to claim her. Marc could never take us to court for claiming our mate. But she'll make her own decision when she wakes up."

"We should hire someone to look after her."

"Yes."

"Just for a little while."

Olivier met Gahariet's eyes. He said, "You're usually a believer in the impossible. Why are you worried about something that might happen? We know who she is. She should know, too."

Olivier walked out of the archive.

Gahariet followed him back to the room where their mysterious mate was sleeping, and he could see that something was different about Phuong's skin in direct sunlight. She was shimmering, almost like the ocean on a sunny day.

He knew that she was their mate. But what happened next was totally up to her. Gahariet didn't like unpredictability — he had enough of it with his twin — but her decision would be incredibly important. They only got one chance at soul mates. If they lost her, they wouldn't be able to get someone who smelled the same as she did, arousing protective instincts from both princes.

He had seen his twin's face in that auction house as he'd helped her out of the cage. He knew that Olivier already felt strongly about her.

Gahariet knew that he was capable of caring for her, but they'd barely met. In contrast, Olivier was someone who threw himself completely into anything at all.

Gahariet always looked before he leapt. He planned things. They were going to marry at least nobility.

And now it seemed that they were blood bound for eternity to a Yore girl. Their father would not be pleased. Their marriage should've been a pre-selected bride, but they'd dodged their duty for long enough.

It was time for them to have a family and produce an heir.

## SIMULACRUM DISCOVERY

### Marc

*A*t the end of the evening's entertainment, Marc went back to check on his most prized possession.

She was asleep inside of her cage. The idea to do surgery right before she came out wasn't his, but he had to admit that it had worked in his favor. She hadn't made any trouble from her cage.

He opened the gate. "Come with me, dear." He knew that his eyes had turned to pure flame.

She took his hand quickly. Without talking, she got to her feet gracefully.

Marc frowned. He came very close to her, his face a half inch from her face.

"Simulacrum," he spat. "Damn it!"

He left the simulacrum in the cage and went running to his office. Inside, one of his seers was downloading his visions.

"You. Come with me."

The seer followed Marc as he ran back to the cage.

"What do you see when you see this woman?"

"Smoke."

Marc's fist hit the cage hard enough to make a sound that would reverberate around the entire room. Pacing around, he couldn't speak because he was so furious.

How dare she escape?

"Why is she so life-like? I couldn't tell before I got close."

"The smoke is royal."

Marc stopped pacing and turned to look at his seer. His Drakan pupils narrowed to vertical slits.

He stood a little straighter.

"They won't be satisfied if they don't have every last thing, will they?"

He snapped his fingers and his body servant appeared. "I want food."

In a minute, food was brought to Marc, a simple steak. His body servant knew better than to ask questions at a time like this. How could he be duped by the twin dragon princes? They were stupid and entitled. How dare they steal from him as if he were some Yore cafard without any power?

They were far too accustomed to the reverence that the lesser Vestrans gave them, deserved or not. None of it was earned. They'd gotten lucky and been born in the right family. They hadn't worked for it, as he had.

He took a sip of his wine and savored it. He was glad that he was in a position to have the finer things in life. Someone needed to challenge them.

That's what he should do. He'd challenge them. He wasn't under their spell, and he didn't need them. They had stolen from the wrong Drakan.

Marc knew what he could do. He went to one of the secret compartments in the room. After the surgery, he'd kept a vial of her blood. It was a small vial which he could use to draw her out. It was much easier than storming a royal castle.

It would be better if she left on her own. From what the Yore seers had told him, the girl was special. She had a great destiny. She was special enough to stay by his side as a mate and mother to his children. She was certainly beautiful enough for the job.

Sparks of fire flickered in front of him as he cast a spell over her blood, whispering that she was his.

He smiled as he felt the whispered message sing in her blood and go faster than light into her mind. It was a time-delayed message, but it would do nicely, lodging in her subconscious until it could break through.

## TEST RESULTS

Gahariet

The next morning, the healer had his tablet in his hand.

"I sent you the results this morning. She's very Yore — I'd say 100% pure Yore, not interbreeding at all. I think that she's an example of what they looked like before the Draka came."

"There were surgical stitches at the base of her head, right next to her neck. I've only seen those kind of scars once before."

"When?" Gahariet asked.

"She must have had some kind of suppression

implant. They put it into Yore that could grow up to be trouble for the Draka."

"You're saying that she's dangerous," Olivier confirmed.

"I'm saying that you should be careful."

The doctor closed his tablet and went to the door.

"I'll have my staff contact you about follow-up visits. We're not sure what will happen when she wakes up."

"You're welcome in the castle at any point that you want. I can get you a permanently valid ID that can get you into our home whenever you like," Gahariet offered

The healer's eyes lit up. "Sounds good to me."

"Then, thank you for your time. We'll take care of all of her medical expenses."

The healer bowed to them before leaving.

"She's pure Yore. Where should we look next?" Olivier asked his brother.

"Birth records," Gahariet replied. The mystery woman still didn't have a proper name.

They walked to the archives in the castle.

They ran an image recognition search on her face, but she wasn't showing up in the genealogical records.

"What kind of person doesn't have a family history?" Olivier said.

"An orphan," Gahariet replied.

"Heritage House," they said simultaneously.

They accessed the records of foundlings who had been raised in Heritage House. The files had no images. Her file had a record of an unsuccessful search for off-planet visitors who had been pregnant while traveling to Vestra, anybody who had visited with small children, and missing citizen reports. But they hadn't been able to find out where she'd come from.

"What is this?" Olivier pointed to a schematic. "This implant?"

Gahariet scanned the file quickly. "Some kind of

suppressant, like the healer said. She was able to mesmerize her handlers at a young age, and when they realized that they didn't want to give her infinite cookies, they suppressed that ability."

"So she has something in her head that keeps her contained?"

"It might be gone. We saw the scars."

Olivier shook his head. "I don't know what that means. She can convince people to do anything?"

"Well, not right now. I'm pretty sure that she's sick, or she would've woken up."

Olivier blew out a long breath. "I need to go for a hunt. I can't stay in here, cooped up and waiting for her to wake up."

"She's fine," Gahariet said. "Why don't we go for a con chim hunt?"

Olivier's eyes lit up. He melted into smoke that poured out of the window, and Gahariet followed him.

Vestra had birds that had the ability to disappear. It was always a surprise to the dragons to crash into the small birds in flight. They were wing-brethren, but it was still fun to chase them. Nobody got hurt. The dragons would often take a single feather from their prey before going away.

The con chim of Vestra were somewhat telepathic with the ability to talk to the dragons inside of their heads. There were myths in the Yore folklore that they could light the sky in times of need, but no Draka had ever seen a light warning.

They circled around the forest until they saw a bird flapping its wings to gain height. They turned and began to chase it. The bird flew frantically, trying to go faster than the dragons, but the dragons gained and gained until suddenly Olivier was swooping down to bite a single feather off of the bird.

*You won.* The bird said. *Now can I go hunt?*

*Go on.* Olivier and Gahariet watched as the bird flew upwards and rode the wind.

Olivier still had the feather in his mouth. Gahariet wouldn't tell him, but it made him look silly. They were a little old to play this hunting game.

They flew back to their own castle, Olivier carefully depositing his hunting trophy on the window sill before flowing back inside as smoke, materializing in human form with a huge grin on his face.

Gahariet was glad that Olivier had a smile on his face again. They knew what the Yore seer had told them would come to pass, but they might as well enjoy themselves while they could.

# WOKEN UP

## Phuong

*P*huong's whole body was warm. She heard the gentle sound of water lapping against the edges of a tub.

Phuong's eyes flew open. Nobody was rich enough to bathe in water.

But she was somehow in a tub of water.

"Oh, you're awake."

She looked downwards. One of the men who had rescued her had a sponge between her thighs. He made a move to withdraw it, but he ended up touching her pleasure core.

She couldn't even control her hips. They bucked upwards, warmth spreading throughout her body, which was very ready to betray her.

She blushed. She was totally naked, and in a bathtub.

Olivier turned his back. "The doctor said that you needed to be clean, even if you were in a coma."

"I wasn't in a coma...was I?"

"Yes, you were. You had a major shock to your system."

She looked at him. She knew that he'd only meant to wash her, but that accidental touch had set her body on fire.

Olivier put the sponge down on the marble countertop.

"Now that you're awake, you can wash yourself. I'll just leave. There's a dressing robe on this hook. We'll talk once you are dressed."

Phuong watched him walk out the door and close it behind him. She was confused about what was happening, but part of her wanted him to come back.

Then she remembered where she was. The twin dragons had rescued her, yes, but now she was in a castle.

There were worse things than taking a bath, though. It seemed like they wanted to take care of her.

Her hand made its way between her thighs to touch the part of her that Olivier had accidentally touched. The water moved with her hips. Closing her eyes, she concentrated on what could've happened if he weren't a gentleman.

*"I WANT YOU,"* he whispered before taking her hard nipple into his mouth and making her cry out as her back arched.

*Her breath was coming in hard pants now. His other hand was rubbing her clitoris in a steady circle with a good rhythm. She could feel the pressure building inside of her body, fire in her veins.*

*Then Olivier bit her neck and forced her into an intense orgasm. Her entire mind was filled with white fire. She could barely breathe.*

PHUONG OPENED HER EYES. What a wild fantasy. She had no idea where that came from. With her orgasm done, she briskly washed her hands and body before getting out. She dried off with a fluffy towel and put on the dressing robe that they'd left for her. It was made out of silk and probably cost enough to feed a Yore family of five for two years, but she shouldn't think about that right now.

When she got out of the bathroom, she saw a raven. It tilted its head at her. She clicked her tongue and tilted her head back. The raven got a little closer to her.

"And what is your name, little con chim?"

"Gregor," a husky voice said behind her.

## STAYING

### Phuong

hirling around, Phuong saw that one of the twins was behind her. Maybe it was the one who bathed her, but she couldn't be sure. The other twin, who looked just like him, was right behind him. How was she supposed to tell them apart?

Her body was humming with energy, her nipples growing hard as she thought about the accidental touch in the tub. She didn't know which one of them had done it, but it had sparked her imagination.

For some reason, she felt drawn to them in a way that she'd never felt drawn to any man before.

"How are you feeling, Phuong?"

"How do you know my name?"

"We have a copy of your record."

She folded her arms over her chest.

"How?"

The raven, Gregor, flew right over to Gahariet.

"Are you hungry?"

They didn't want to answer her question.

"How did you find my record?"

"It doesn't matter. Let's get breakfast."

"You can't keep me here. I don't owe you any debts or anything. I'm grateful that you broke me out of that cage, but..."

"Don't worry. We only want to see that you're in good condition. Would you be so kind as to agree to spend the rest of the day with us to talk about... well...some things?"

When Olivier had bound them with blood, he hadn't thought about talking. But Gahariet seemed more open.

"The rest of the day, and then I can go?"

"You can go now," Gahariet said, "but we'd like to spend more time with you."

"Just today, then."

"Sounds good. Are you comfortable in your robe?"

She looked down. The cloth was thin, but it was comfortable.

"I'm just fine."

"Then let us show you around the castle."

Gahariet left the room. She trailed him uncertainly. She'd never been inside of a Drakan castle before.

There was a very musty smell, as if nobody ever dusted in here, although she knew that they had dozens of Yore servants. There were Drakan castles with hundreds of Yore servants.

If they had a castle, they were Thrones, the top

level of prince-hood. The Drakans had several different degrees of prince-hood before you got diluted enough to be just a noble.

Each of the families had different sections of Vestra to rule. The planet was more than large enough for each Drakan prince to have his own area.

The Thrones especially had ancient and modern treasures tucked away in their stronghold. She had to admit, as they slowly made their way through the entire castle, that she wanted to look for the jewels, ancient coins, golden statues, and precious minerals that they had in their hoard.

But she didn't get anywhere near them. Even though she was a guest in their home, it was hard to be in the same place as so much wealth and not take anything. Even one golden cup would be able to feed them for a year.

But now she could smell food. Her stomach grumbled. She put her hand over her lower stomach, totally embarrassed.

"We should've fed you. You've been asleep for a while. You should've said something."

Olivier abruptly changed course. The smell of food grew stronger.

Suddenly, she was in heaven.

She could see food everywhere. There were at least a dozen people in the kitchen, maybe even more.

"You'll have to wait until dinner for the fancy stuff, but we can have a simple meal right now."

Olivier grabbed a loaf of fresh bread and a little bowl of butter from the cold storage.

"How about a little wine?"

"Isn't it a little early in the day?" Phuong didn't know much about drinking.

"Wine with every meal!" Olivier poured some wine into wine glasses.

They had simple, crusty bread with some divine garlic-flavored butter.

"What's in this?"

"Garlic and cinnamon."

Phuong choked. "What?"

"It's not an intuitive combination, but it's dynamite. Before the Draka came to Vestra, we didn't understand how to use cinnamon in savory dishes. The Yore use it, and honestly, this butter is from one of our servants."

Phuong felt the food sit in her stomach like a stone. She was eating the product of the Drakan overlords' oppression of her people, the Yore.

Even their simple food was luxurious for someone like her. The whole kitchen was full of good things to eat. They had an easy and decadent life on the back of the conquered Yore.

Her face heated. She wished that she hadn't agreed to stay with them for the day.

# SENSITIVE

## Phuong

She should've just run at the first chance that they'd given her. They couldn't keep an eye on her every second of the day. Or maybe she should've just been firm about leaving.

But she had to admit that her senses were definitely heightened and on edge when she was around the Draka Thrones. She felt strangely compelled to stay, as if she belonged here.

"Why don't you drink some of your wine? It's Intaran Spätburgunder."

She drank a sip of the red wine. It helped calm her down.

"We wanted to talk to you about what the medical tests showed."

"Medical tests?"

"We had to run some on you when we got you. You were unconscious. A healer ran a full battery of tests on you."

"What did they say?"

"They said that you're pure-blooded Yore, not a drop of Draka in you."

"Yup, low-born Yore." What was she doing in this castle? She crossed her arms around herself. She wasn't the kind of girl who could just hang out with any Draka, let alone Thrones.

"No, you aren't low-born at all."

"What?"

"You're not even a Yore merchant. Your blood is old, and you definitely didn't fit into Heritage House, or they never would have implanted you with a suppression device."

Phuong felt the scar at the base of her skull.

"Oh?"

Gahariet said, "Your magical influence is going to become more prominent. Your senses should feel sharper now. Your children are going to be extraordinary. Yore can give birth to more than one child at a time, just like Drakans can. But your child will be even more special with Olivier's DNA in you."

Phuong felt her cheeks turn completely red.

Olivier cough-laughed. "He didn't mean it like that. He was talking about my blood."

"Oh." Phuong's cheeks cooled a little. "Well, that would be impossible, anyway. We haven't...I haven't...we've never..." Her cheeks got hot again.

"We can fix that, if you like."

"Oh...no..." Phuong got to her feet and ran out of the kitchen as fast as she could.

When she got to the corridor, she ran straight into a hard body. Somebody's hands came to her elbows, steadying her on her feet.

Then she looked up, way up, at Olivier's face.

"How did you?"

"We're dragons," he said gently. "We can turn into smoke."

"Oh," Phuong said, blinking. There wasn't going to be a time when she'd be able to run away from people who could easily teleport.

"Are we really so bad?" Gahariet asked. "Why don't you want to mate with us?" He was behind her. She felt his hard erection pressed gently against her backside.

A thrumming began in her lower parts. She could feel herself getting damp, her muscles relaxing just a hair.

"I don't...I've never..."

"We would make it good for you," Gahariet whispered in her ear. His hands were on the lower curve of her soft stomach, and then they were just a little lower.

Olivier got even closer and put his hand under her chin so that she was staring straight into his eyes, his mouth not even a breath away.

"Just say yes," Olivier said. "Say yes, and you'll experience something better than anything you've known before."

Phuong was sandwiched between the two dragons, feeling one erection pressing into the soft curves of her bottom and the other one digging just a little bit into her stomach.

"Yes," she said, surrendering. Maybe it was the sip of alcohol, but she felt pleasantly loose and warm.

Olivier's mouth came crashing down on hers, like a dragon swooping down on its prey. His kiss tasted like wine, like pouring warm wine down her throat.

His hands went to the curves of her hips. Gahariet's hands were cupping her breasts now, playing with them as his brother explored Phuong's mouth.

Then Olivier's hands were at the back of her head, and he touched her recent surgery's scar. Shooting pain radiated from the base of her skull.

"Ouch," she said, and the moment shattered like untempered glass. She stepped out from between them. She looked from Olivier to Gahariet, feeling naked and vulnerable in front of them. She could see the fire in their eyes, and she didn't know how she should be feeling.

"My brother. I need to see him. He needs to know that I'm okay. I...I'm tired. I need to rest." She walked in a daze deeper into the castle. How was she going to last a whole day in this castle with them?

# POOL GAME

## Gahariet

Olivier took the pool cue in his hands and shot the cue ball as hard as he could.

But the pool table wasn't meant to be abused by a Drakan at full strength. The ball went spinning out of control. The tip of the pool cue hit the blue fabric, ripping through it and ruining the table. It was a gift from an ambassador of a country that Gahariet couldn't remember.

"Ugh," he said, throwing his stick down on the ground.

He turned to Gahariet. "This may not have been the best way to let off steam."

"We need to give her some time. She's just overwhelmed, that's all."

"Maybe we made a mistake when we chose her."

"You know that we didn't. She's ours."

Gahariet knew that Olivier just needed to simmer down. All the time, he was the hotter burning flame, especially after their mother had passed.

But now he was burning hotter than before. Gahariet knew that it was hard for Olivier to open up emotionally, and he'd already started forming a romantic attachment to Phuong. To be rebuffed so early on was crushing.

His dragon mind couldn't understand why their mate would push them away. Gahariet had a tighter grip on his dragon nature, and he knew that they just needed to give Phuong time to adjust.

His attraction to her — and Olivier's attraction to her — was primal. She wasn't a dragon, though, and she didn't have a second mind inside of her.

Gahariet knew in his bones that she would be their queen. On some level, surely she knew about it.

They just needed to let her accept that she would be by their side.

"I need to get outside." With that, Olivier dissolved in smoke.

Gahariet just sighed. They would all process their new binding in their own ways.

# NIGHTMARE

## Phuong

*P*huong woke up when she heard a piercing scream. Distantly, she realized that she was the one who was screaming.

She saw that Gregor, their raven, was at the foot of her bed. The twins were coming through her door, materializing in human form. They rushed to her bed as if they knew her well enough to come into her bed at night.

How long had she slept? She'd only meant to take a short nap before going to find her brother at the end of the day.

She suddenly realized just how intimate this

moment was. Both of them were in her bedroom. But sex wasn't on their mind. Olivier was reaching for her hand and Gahariet was perched on the edge of the bed. They wanted to take care of her.

"What happened? What's wrong?"

"My brother."

"We'll find him, don't worry."

"You can't find him."

"Fate will bring him here. Your blood has mixed with ours. Blood calls to blood."

Phuong was silent for a moment. "I hope so."

"Anything else happen?"

"I had a really bad nightmare."

"Yeah?"

"In it, the auction master, Marc, told me that I belonged to him. He said that he'd get me back and keep me forever."

Gahariet frowned at her. "He must have some of your blood."

"What? Why would he need my blood? What are you talking about?"

"He must have gotten into your mind with some of your blood when they did that surgery. He can reach into your head. He'll try other things if he still has more blood."

Gahariet was looking at Olivier now.

"There were other...dreams?"

"What were they?"

Phuong felt cold in her bed. She wrapped her arms around herself.

"I saw a nation of ghosts, Yore ancestors. They told me to watch where I stepped."

"Of course, they were talking about Marc," Gahariet said.

"They told me that I was a princess, but that can't be right. I'm nobody."

"You're a princess...our princess and a future queen. You're definitely somebody." Olivier reached for her and brought her close, tucking her head on his shoulder, careful not to touch the back of her head this time. His hand stroked her back in slow circles.

"We didn't tell you yet, but you're probably a Yore princess."

"What!" Phuong pulled away from Olivier's warm and wonderfully solid body. "What are you talking about?"

"We talked about the fact that you were 100% Yore before," Gahariet said in a matter-of-fact tone.

"Yeah."

"Well, you might be a Yore princess," Olivier revealed.

"Why would I be given away if I have royal blood?"

Phuong shook her head. It didn't make any sense at all. She and her brother had scrabbled to stay alive. What king or queen would do that to their babies?

Phuong bit her lip. They were just spinning her a tale, dangling the idea that she could be a princess in her own right to convince her to stay with them and be their princess...the mother of their children.

She put her hand on her stomach. There was a part of her that would love to have their dragon children.

But they were just too wealthy. She wasn't meant to be with a Throne, let alone two. They could buy anything and anyone that they wanted. Besides, she didn't know what exactly they wanted.

"Just quiet your mind and listen to your heart. You know who you are, deep down. We will support you in any way that you need, because we're bound, heart, mind, and soul, forever."

"You'll see it if you just open yourself to the possibilities."

What did they know about optimism? They'd lived a charmed life. They always had enough money. They hadn't had to escape from an orphanage and scratch out a living.

Phuong glared at them, but she said nothing.

Gahariet was aware enough to know to back off, so he got to his feet and grabbed the back of Olivier's sleep shirt.

"We'll leave you to rest. Just yell if you need us."

"But I..."

Gahariet pulled Olivier out of the room.

"Goodnight, Phuong."

## WANDERING

Phuong

*W*hen Phuong woke up the next morning, she realized that she hadn't left, as she'd intended to. The nightmare had definitely thrown her plans off.

As she got out of bed, she yelped at the feeling of the cold stone floor. Of course dragons would live in stone castles. Wood was a bad idea.

What was it like to raise a baby dragon? She might never know. She was Yore through and through. Now that her implant was gone, she needed to explore the side of herself that had been locked away for so long. There had been a black spot in her mind for a long time. In her most vulnerable moments, she asked the stars to get rid of the implant.

And now, not only was the implant gone, but she was told that she was a princess — a royal Yore.

She didn't know if she believed the dragon twins. She felt drawn to them, sure, but she didn't know if she was ready to mate them for life. She wasn't that old. But she was afraid that her body, which got a little wet when they were near, would push her towards accepting the two of them as her mates.

She threw open the wardrobe in her beautiful room and put on one of her dresses. She had too many, more than she could ever reasonably wear, and she chose the one on the end, blue with silver and green shot through it. At least the silver matched her hair.

She pulled it over her head before going down the stairs. She followed her nose to the breakfast room.

As soon as she entered it, an attendant poured a glass of wine at her table. She had only just sat down when the twin dragons came into the room.

She turned as they stopped in their tracks, apparently astonished to see her there.

Gahariet recovered first, giving her a grin.

"Good morning, gorgeous. How are you feeling?"

"Better. Much better." She looked at the attendant, who took his cue and left the room.

Gahariet came in to brush her cheek lightly with his hand. "No more nightmares?"

"None." She smiled up at him. "Silly to be afraid of ghosts."

"It's okay," Olivier said. "I have nightmares with the ghost of my mom sometimes."

Gahariet backed up a step. "What?"

"Yup."

"I've never heard about those."

"I don't share every single detail of my life with you, Gahariet." Olivier reached for his plate and began to eat.

All of them dedicated themselves to eating. Phuong was done with her meal within 10 minutes. She watched as the dragons went back for second and third helpings. It seemed that dragons ate a lot.

They were tall humans, yeah, but dragons were big. Where did all that extra mass come from? She felt too shy to ask them about it.

She sat there, drinking her wine and feeling a little bit tipsy. She didn't have much experience with alcohol. She had to admit that she liked drinking wine with breakfast. It made the day just a little bit brighter.

Gahariet got to his feet.

"Do you like jazz?"

"Yes, of course. Who doesn't?"

Gahariet waved his hand. Soft jazz music filled the room.

"Would you dance with me, Princess?"

She put her hand in his, drawn to him just like a magnet. She looked up at his face. His hands rested together at the small of her back. Every bit of her curves was pressed against his hard body.

And then he began to move. Slowly and softly at first, but with perfect confidence, he pulled her into the steps of a dance that she didn't know.

And then he was twirling her, and at the end of the spin, somehow she was in Olivier's arms.

He gripped her by the waist and spun her in a quick circle above his head. It was exhilarating to be spun around like this.

Then he brought her to the ground, letting her feet touch the ground for a mere instant before he bent her body backwards and kissed her deeply.

His tongue was cold and firm, pushing inside of her. And then she felt like fire was being unleashed from him, like it was filling her whole body, like she was burning up in a red-hot blaze. She felt weak at the knees.

Her legs stopped supporting her then, but she was fine, because Olivier's strong arms held her up.

Then she was suddenly vertical, her arms still wrapped around Olivier's broad shoulders. She felt the warmth of Gahariet's body pressing close to her, his erection now pressing against the lowest part of her back.

Olivier stopped kissing her.

"Come back!" she complained. "I wasn't done."

"Oh, baby, you're far from done." Olivier slid to his knees. He raised her skirt and touched his tongue to the soft skin at the very top of her inner thigh.

Her knees gave way then, but Gahariet was there to catch her and support her. His muscular arms were under her armpits, one hand gripping a breast and stroking it gently.

Oliver was very skilled with his tongue. He knew the right buttons to press as he touched her and lapped at her with perfectly rhythmic strokes. She felt her body go higher and higher.

Then he pushed a thick, long finger inside of her. Her whole body felt like it was exploding in a gigantic fireball.

And then she went supernova.

SUPERNOVA

Phuong

*W*hen she came back to herself, drifting down from her orgasm, she was kissing Gahariet. His cool tongue pushed its way inside of her mouth, but his fiery body made her warm. His hands were pinning her wrists to the table. Her back arched as she writhed beneath him, fire flooding her whole body and melting every part of it.

"You ready?"

"Yes," she moaned, thrusting her hips towards him. "Take me."

She felt the broad head of his cock pushing against

her untouched entrance. His hands were pulling her thighs further apart.

"I need you to relax, okay? I'm big, but I won't hurt you. I want you to relax all the muscles in your body."

He leaned down to kiss her cleavage. Her lower lips clenched, and then they relaxed. He stroked her soft lower lips with his hand.

"Good."

Then his cock was back at her entrance again. His mouth came down to bite her shoulder as he claimed her for the first time.

Her body burned with incredible heat. It felt as if he had taken a burning poker from a fireplace and pushed it inside of her, but it burned in the most pleasurable way imaginable.

Her eyes were closed. She could hear the sound of Gahariet's skin slapping against her own.

Then she smelled Olivier getting close to her. Her sense of smell was somehow better now. She opened her eyes and got an eyeful of his erection.

"My turn. Open wide."

Before she could say anything, he guided himself inside of her mouth.

He tasted salty, like the best thing that she'd ever eaten.

"Mmm," she said around his cock. His balls slapped against her chin as he began to claim her mouth just as fiercely as his brother was claiming Phuong's lower body.

"I'm not going to last," Olivier gasped. "Oh, stars, so good."

"Uh," Gahariet said. Phuong felt like a fireball had been unleashed inside of her. "I'm about to come."

And then Gahariet let out another groan. This time, Phuong felt as if her body was placed on an exploding star. She came apart into a thousand pieces. She might have orgasmed before, but that was like comparing a candle to a giant sun. She cried out around Olivier's cock, which slid even deeper, touching the beginning of her throat.

"I don't think that she has a gag reflex."

Olivier slid even deeper inside of her throat.

"I'm gonna..."

And then he unleashed himself inside of her. Her mouth was so full that it overflowed with his essence, spilling onto her cheeks. She swallowed as much as she could, but it was difficult to get much since Olivier was blocking the passageway.

"Uh!" Olivier said, slamming back inside of her. He filled her with a second shot.

Then he pulled out of her mouth.

As soon as Olivier was clear, Gahariet pulled Phuong into his arms.

"We should take you to a nice, soft bed." He leaned down and kissed her neck, making her body aroused yet again.

## RIPPED DRESS

Gahariet

He looked down at his precious mate in his arms. He almost wished that he didn't have to share her with his brother, but he always would. The three of them were one, now and forever.

He ran up the stairs, Olivier close behind. They went into his room. He was glad that he had a dragon-sized bed.

He threw his precious cargo down on his bed before climbing on top of her body. He wanted access to her luscious breasts.

So he gripped the neckline of her dress and tore it

in half, exposing every inch of her dark skin. His tongue lapped at one of her hard nipples. His hand went between her thighs, gathering the creamy wetness and pushing two fingers inside of her body while his thumb circled around and around her clit.

Then it was time to change positions. He'd kept her delicious body to himself for long enough.

He quickly flipped her onto her stomach to take off the remnants of her dress. Then she was totally naked in his bed.

Pulling her hip so that her back was to his front, Olivier slid in front of her, while Gahariet lifted her top leg and put it on top of his brother's outer thigh, bending her leg at the knee.

She gasped a little bit when Olivier slid inside of her body. Gahariet put his hand on her clit to rub her as his brother claimed her.

Her body was shaking so much that she was shaking the bed.

Gahariet's hand was wet with her juices. He

brought the juices to her back door, slowly sliding the wetness around the dark hole.

"Are you...?" she asked.

"Just relax," he said quietly. "Relax."

Olivier leaned in and bit her neck. She yelped loudly. Her butt flexed and Olivier groaned as he began to thrust into her a little more quickly.

"Hold on," Gahariet told Olivier. "We're going to double up on her."

"Hurry up," Olivier said through clenched teeth. "She feels so good. I don't think I'm going to last."

Gahariet took as much wetness as he could and then he put the tip of cock into her hole.

She was insanely tight.

"Relax," he said quietly into her little ear. He dropped a tender kiss on her cheek before biting her earlobe.

Slowly, she eased around him. And then he was pushing past her sphincter.

The whole room smelled of vanilla, salt, and musk. Gahariet gathered one of her soft, luscious breasts in his hand, squeezing gently to maximize her pleasure.

"I feel so full," she said.

"We've barely started." Gahariet slid deeper.

"Oh," she moaned. "So much."

Olivier couldn't hold on anymore. His hands gripped her hips so hard that his knuckles were turning white.

His eyes were closed as he drove into her again and again, trying to find his completion.

And his twin was releasing inside of her little body. A heartbeat later, Olivier pulled out of her.

And then she was Gahariet's. He pushed her until she was flat on her stomach, and she moved to pull her thighs apart.

"No," he told her. "I like you tight like this." He pushed her legs together.

He gathered her wrists into one of his hands and held them against the bed above her head.

"Let me help you," Olivier said, replacing Gahariet's grip with his own.

Gahariet was free to put his hands on her smooth, soft shoulders with his knees on either side of her body.

And then he was going wild on top of her small body, giving everything that he could to her. She took everything like a champion. He could see from the rapid rise and fall of her back that she was breathing hard.

One of his hands went from her shoulder to circle her delicate neck. He closed his hand just a little. He could feel her heart beating like a rabbit's from the pulse in her neck.

"Come for me," he commanded. "Fly."

With a scream, she shuddered below him, her hand whipping around wildly as her body shook its way through another orgasm. He could feel the tension in her below him.

And then the clenching of her body pushed him to his own completion. He released inside of his blood-bound mate like he had an unlimited supply of seed inside of him, pulsing again and again, filling her beyond her capacity.

But finally, his body stopped releasing, and he eased himself out of his mate.

He rolled them to their side again, Olivier sliding in front of her. Gahariet arranged her thigh on top of Olivier's again.

Gahariet knew that they should get clean, but somehow he didn't have the energy to handle it. His eyes were closing, even though it was still morning.

# REMEDY

## Phuong

*P*huong felt something cold pressed against her forehead. She could see bits of light even though her eyes were closed.

"She's processing."

"The dragon blood will help. Give her some more."

She tasted the iron taste of dragon blood in her mouth.

Fire burst inside of her body, making it feel like her skin was too tight for her. She tossed and turned, her eyes still closed, writhing on the bed where her lovers had claimed all of her virginity.

Something about love-making made her feel like there were cords binding her to them. She was closer to their thoughts like this. She could practically feel their minds with hers. She knew that even if they were in a crowd, she'd be able to find them, even if she couldn't see.

She felt like they were inside of her. Feeling safe, she let herself drift off again.

\* \* \*

SHE BLINKED AWAKE LATER. She felt a surge of power inside of her. A light was on near her.

Ghariet's smooth voice said, "It's okay. Relax. Everything is okay."

Her eyes finally opened. She could see his face. He was sitting in a chair next to her. He put his hand in hers.

She drifted back to sleep.

\* \* \*

WHEN SHE WOKE up yet again, she saw that

Olivier was next to her.

"We have some tea for you."

"I don't really like tea."

"It's an old Drakan family recipe to help you adjust."

She accepted the mug from Olivier and took a sip. She felt it douse her inner fire just a little.

"What's happening to me?"

"Your body is getting used to the dragon blood, that's all."

"So my symptoms are normal?"

"They're to be expected, yeah."

She stared at him, feeling a tug inside of her pulling her towards him. She got to her knees, then she was pulling him close and sealing his mouth with hers.

With her tongue in his mouth, she could feel him. All of him. Every bit of his pain and frustration. All of his joy, the razor blade of loss that cut him every day that he didn't have his mother.

"You aren't alone, Olivier. You have me." She kissed him again, lightly and sweetly. She had no idea why she'd said that, but the words had flowed out of her as if from her sleeping mind.

Olivier was extroverted, but he still held a part of him apart from other people, including his own twin. But she could feel his feelings when she was on top of him.

She wondered why she hadn't noticed before. Was it because she couldn't do it during sex or did she just not notice because there was so much going on?

Pushing her way inside of him again, she instantly felt everything that he felt, everything that he was made up of.

She felt the raging fire, all-consuming and ever-burning.

This time, he was the one to pull back.

"I'll get Gahariet. Wait here."

She touched her kiss-swollen lips. "I'll be right here," she promised.

# CABIN FEVER

Phuong

The next day, she was bored out of her mind. Her cabin fever was growing by leaps and bounds. The twins had wanted her to stay in the castle until she was better. She felt a lot better, and she needed to leave.

She went to the kitchen to ask the cook a question.

"Excuse me?"

"Yes?" The cook took out a knife and chopped a head of lettuce. "How can I help you?"

Phuong eyed the enormous knife. "I was just wondering where the twins were."

"They went to Assembly. They'll be back late afternoon. Do you want breakfast?"

"Yes, please."

"There's a fruit basket over there." The cook motioned with her head, since her hands were full. "Anything else?"

"Nope, that's it. Thank you." Phuong went over and grabbed an apple out of the basket before leaving the kitchen.

She walked around the castle solo. She came to a door that she'd never seen before. It was very tall and had iron bars on it.

She opened the door and found herself in a room full of books, a library. The books were antiquated, of course, but she still liked the smell.

Did they have any books that would tell about her abilities? The removal of her implant had sparked more questions than ever. She didn't know herself.

Even though Gahariet and Olivier made her feel welcome in their castle, she wished that she knew who she was. And Xuan would need to know, too, if she could just find him.

She hoped that he was safe in their den. She missed him like a fifth limb, and she knew that she wanted to see him and send word to him as soon as she could. She was beginning to fall in love with the princes, but she also wasn't a fool. Phuong wasn't about to tell them where her safe haven was. If they ever turned on her, she would be left without a place to flee to. And she couldn't go herself yet, just in case they had guards that would track her.

Since she'd just been sick with the transition, she was going to go earlier than her mates would permit, but that meant figuring a way out of the castle that her mates and none of the Yore staff would notice.

She heard a clicking sound and left the library. The clicking was almost a tune, a hypnotic lullaby. Her steps were slow, going to the beat of the tune. She felt like there was a lasso around her middle, pulling her out of the castle.

"Where are you going? You're supposed to stay in here."

But Phuong swept past the door attendant.

"Hey! Aren't you sick? Come back!"

Even though Phuong wanted to turn back, she couldn't.

All of a sudden, the air around her was full with dozens of butterflies.

Pretty. She reached out her hand, mesmerized by the patterns on their wings.

"Phuong!" Gahariet shouted.

She snapped out of her butterfly and tune-induced daze. She saw one man dressed in black running away. Was he there to snatch her?

"Did you not notice that there was a team of mercenaries trying to grab you?"

"No...the music...the butterflies." She couldn't really understand what had happened.

"Let's get you inside," Gahariet said softly. Olivier was behind Gahariet. The three went back inside.

## LAGOON

### Olivier

*O*livier watched Phuong slide into the water of their private lagoon. Her eyes were closed, her face showing that she was immersing herself in pure ecstasy.

He'd seen Yore like this before. He'd always wondered why something as simple as water would bliss them out. She looked like she was orgasming, pleasure taking over her body.

Stars, she was beautiful. Her dark skin was glowing slightly in the sunlight. He stood by the shore and watched his mate relax in the lagoon for a while before he felt his twin approach behind him.

"What are we going to do about Marc?" Gahariet asked his twin.

Olivier turned. "Do we have to do anything? I mean, we're safe inside of our own grounds and castle. We should be able to protect her."

"He has her blood. He clearly wants to use it to control her." Gahariet was frowning.

"She doesn't belong to him."

"He's not going to accept our claim."

"I don't care." Olivier's fists were clenched.

"You should care. As long as someone like Marc wants her, she's not going to be safe."

Olivier turned and glared at his brother, who took a step back. Gahariet took a second step back and put his hands up.

"Pursuing her any longer wouldn't be safe for Marc," he told him, menace clear in his voice.

"We'll do the best we can, but there aren't any guarantees. And we still don't know where her brother is." Gahariet shook his head.

"We can find Xuan, I'm sure. It's not safe for him to be on the streets, not when Marc is out there. We just need a little more time, that's all."

"I don't know if we need more time to find him. He's pretty well hidden. Do you think that our mate knows where he is hiding?"

Both of them looked at their floating mate, whose eyes were still closed.

"We'll do everything we can to keep her safe. What if she's pregnant with our babies?" Gahariet asked.

"I don't know what would happen if he kidnapped her while she was pregnant."

"Well, I don't want to find out."

"He's not going to touch her," Olivier promised.

Gahariet shook his head. "I've got to get back to work. I'll talk to you both later." Gahariet left the lagoon, leaving Olivier and Phuong alone.

Olivier shucked off his clothes. The Draka didn't care much about nudity, and he didn't mind getting a little dirt on him.

He waded into the water, then he began to float

next to Phuong. It had been a long time since Olivier had taken the time to just float around... maybe a decade. Maybe more.

Her eyes were still closed, but she reached her hand out to him. The two of them floated together in the pool in a perfect moment of peace and silence, a stark contrast to the kidnapping attempt that Marc had perpetrated.

Olivier wished that their peace could last forever, but he knew that it wouldn't.

# DEMAND

## Gahariet

Gahariet went back to his office. He looked at his twin's empty seat and shook his head. Olivier would dodge his responsibilities as often as he could. He lived for the moment, which for him meant spending as much time with Phuong as possible.

Gahariet supposed that someone needed to watch Phuong, so he didn't mind going through all the paperwork on his own.

Today, the paperwork seemed even more boring than usual. There were a bunch of Assembly arbitration decisions that he had to make. He shuffled through them, sighing. Sometimes, being the responsible twin meant that he was inside a lot more often than his brother was.

There was one envelope that wasn't like the others. It had the Alrech Auction House wax seal on it, the wax as red as blood.

He took a slender letter opener and opened the envelope.

In crimson ink, Marc had written: "Return my property."

Gahariet tossed the letter down on his desk. Phuong was more than just a valuable auction item. She was a Yore princess in her own right. She was a wonder and a mystery. Above all of those things, she was their beloved blood-bound mate.

Fate itself had determined their path. The three of them belonged together. It wasn't an accident that they had been in the auction house on the same night. If they hadn't come by... Phuong would still be trapped with Marc, probably. Stars only knew what he would've done to her.

Gahariet ran through the possibilities in his mind.

He hoped that the fight wouldn't have to get nasty — he was a royal, after all — but he would do what it took to protect his mate, no matter what the cost.

Gahariet was lost in thought when he heard the door of his office slam open.

"She's sleeping," Olivier announced.

"I got a letter," Gahariet said softly. "Maybe you should read it."

"A letter?"

"From Marc." Gahariet pointed.

"Let me see."

He reached for the letter that Gahariet indicated was from Marc.

Olivier read the single sentence there and snorted. "Phuong is not his property."

"It means that he's discovered that the simulacrum isn't her."

"Good. Then I can just let it dissolve. It was taking a lot of energy, anyway." Olivier closed his eyes. "It's gone now, just so much smoke."

"Not everything about this is going to be resolved that easily, Olivier," Gahariet warned.

"Marc can bring it. He thinks that he can take on two Thrones? Ridiculous. We will crush him."

Gahariet didn't sigh, even though he wanted to. His brother thought that if you fought as hard as you could, you'd always win. Gahariet was his twin, but he knew that even if they gave it everything they had, it was possible that they could lose.

Marc had shadowy connections to the underground market, which Gahariet didn't like at all. The black market was unregulated and beyond their control.

"I'm starving," Olivier complained. "Do you want to grab something downstairs?"

"Why don't we eat in Phuong's room?"

Olivier licked his lips. "Mm, I am pretty hungry."

Gahariet shook his head. His brother loved getting sweaty.

Gahariet did, too, of course, but he didn't need it

the way that Olivier did. He had a reputation as a playboy prince which was very well deserved.

"I'll meet you there in ten. Can you grab the food?"

"Sure."

Olivier walked out of the room while Gahariet arranged all of the paper in proper stacks. It was true that technology could keep everything much more orderly, but the older Draka were used to printing things physically, and they highly preferred actual paper for legal proceedings.

Gahariet tucked everything away properly before going to Phuong's room.

# FEVERISH

## Gahariet

As Gahariet approached her room, he could hear the sound of his twin's voice. "Your eyes are red."

"Are they?" Phuong sounded startled. Gahariet began to walk faster towards her room.

Then he heard the thump of something hitting a headboard. He broke into a full-out run.

When he got into the room, Phuong was in Olivier's arms. He was checking her head.

"She's going to have a big bump there."

"What happened?"

"She fainted. Feel her. She's burning up."

Gahariet reached out, stopping with his hand only a half inch from her forehead. But then he finally connected with her and he saw what his twin had been talking about. Her inner fire was consuming her. Her body had no idea how to regulate her temperature as the dragon blood mingled with hers.

"We can't keep her here. We've got to cool her down."

"Ice?"

"No, water. The Yore feel the best in water." Olivier stood with their mate in his arms. "I think that I have to carry her down. If I carry her in my claws, I might drop her or hurt her."

"Why don't we put her in a cart and wheel her down together?" Honestly, Olivier never planned ahead. With an ounce of foresight, the journey to their private lagoon would be much faster.

"That's a good idea."

Gahariet went to a nearby storage closet and pulled out a wooden cart. He made a face, because it smelled musty, as if nobody had used it for a while. But he went back to Phuong's room. He took the blanket from her bed before Olivier set Phuong down gently inside of the cart.

"How are we going to get the cart down the stairs?" Olivier asked.

"We're going to just carry her instead of wheeling her down."

Gahariet picked up the front of the cart and walked backwards, carefully stepping down the stairs one by one.

When they were at the bottom, they slowly set the cart on its wheels and began to pull their mate towards the lagoon.

They didn't anticipate quite how bumpy the ground would be. It jolted her unconscious body over and over again. Gahariet gritted his teeth. It turned out that his plans weren't necessarily the best, after all.

But then they were finally there. Olivier picked her up.

"So how are we going to do this? Just throw her in?" Olivier asked.

"She's unconscious, so, no." Gahariet pulled her body from Olivier's arms. "We're going to just walk in with her."

"We're fully dressed," Olivier protested.

"Do you care about ruining your clothes?"

"Not really, not right now."

"Then walk in with me." Gahariet walked into the cool water of the lagoon. He was relieved to feel that Phuong's body temperature instantly got a little lower.

"How long is her molting going to last?"

"I have no idea. I know that some of the Yore-Draka mixes turn into dragons, but I don't know what it's like if you're full Yore, like she is," Gahariet admitted.

"Do you think that it could hurt?"

"It might. I have no clue."

"Do you think that it's worth it?" Olivier asked.

"Of course. She's our mate. She's going to be a dragon." Gahariet shook his head.

"Ah," Phuong moaned. Gahariet looked at his semi-conscious mate. Her eyelids were fluttering quite a bit.

"Puzzle," she sighed.

"What did she say?" Olivier said.

"She said 'puzzle'," Gahariet responded. "And look—she's getting her scales."

She shifted in Gahariet's arms, so he adjusted his position. She was a little lighter in the water, but it also made her slippery.

"Scales?" Olivier leaned in to her skin. "She was getting shiny before."

He ran his hands over her skin, which seemed a little rougher than it had been before. "It's like a scale pattern more than anything, not full-on scales."

"It's still exciting."

Gahariet touched Phuong's skin, too. It was starting to change just a little bit.

"I hope she doesn't have a fever the whole time."

"She should be fine in the lagoon, though, right?" Olivier was frowning at his twin. "It's not dangerous?"

"It shouldn't be," Gahariet replied, but he wasn't so sure.

## WARMING UP

### Phuong

*P*huong opened her eyes. What strange dreams she'd had. Finally, everything had fit together perfectly.

Why was she wet? Her body felt hot on the inside, but cold on the outside.

She looked up at Gahariet's sculpted face above her.

"How do you feel, sweetheart?"

"I..." She flexed her hands and then her feet. "I'm okay."

"You have scales now," Olivier told her.

"What?"

"Look at your hands."

Phuong realized that Gahariet was holding her up. She lifted a hand towards her face and looked closely. Sure enough, there was some kind of scale pattern beneath her skin.

"I'm a dragon?"

"You're turning into one, a very beautiful one."

Phuong frowned. Other than feeling hot, she didn't feel that different.

"Am I going to be half shifted like this forever?"

"No. You'll be able to control it with some practice."

"But right now, I'm going to have scales?"

"It looks like it," Gahariet said. "We don't have definite answers, but I can tell you that we'll be with you every step of the way. Now why don't we go back to the castle and pump you full of fluids? We've immersed you in the lagoon, but you could dry out from the inside, and that's not good.

Dehydration can be a major problem during transition."

Gahariet began walking out of the lagoon. Phuong clung to him and threw her arms around his neck, her head against his chest.

She shivered when she was out of the water. Her teeth were chattering.

"Why is it so cold?"

"The contrast between the outside temperature and your inner fire makes it feel cold. Dragons are cold-blooded anyway. We'll take you home and get you out of your wet clothes."

Gahariet set her down gently in the wooden cart. All three of them were wearing wet clothes as they set off for home.

They only went a little way before Olivier stopped. "I hate this shirt," Olivier said before stripping it off and putting it over his arm.

"It's not that comfortable," Gahariet agreed before whipping off his own shirt.

Phuong tried not to stare, but both of the brothers

had perfect musculature, their broad shoulders were probably twice the size of hers. Then their backs tapered into a perfect V-shape at their slim hips. She had an amazing view as they pulled her in the cart up the castle. She was perfectly capable of walking, but she'd rather sit in this cart, no matter how much it jolted her.

Then they had gone all the way up the path and were at the castle.

Gahariet helped Phuong out of the cart before stowing it beside the door.

"Someone will know what to do with it," Gahariet said. "Now, do you want to drink some hot xocolatl or get changed?"

"I need to change," Phuong said, gesturing at her dress ruefully. "I'm afraid it's a little more scandalous for me to take off my dress than it is for you to take off your shirts."

"Well, I wouldn't be scandalized," Olivier teased. "You can take off your dress in front of me anytime."

Phuong blushed, which helped warm her up a little bit. The three of them went to her room.

Gahariet said, "Give me your dress. I can send it down to our laundry room. It can be as good as new."

Phuong looked at her beautiful dress. "Okay." She bit her lip. "Could you two turn your backs?"

"No," Olivier said bluntly. "You're our mate. We've had sex. If you want to see us naked, too, we can go first." Olivier stripped off all of his clothing so that he was naked. "Besides, I think that I heard that the best way to warm someone up was skin-to-skin contact."

"Sounds good to me." Gahariet took off his clothes, too, draping them on a chair in her room. "Come on, Phuong, don't you want to be warm?"

Phuong looked between the two dragons. Both were aroused and coming towards her. What did she want?

She tugged the hem of her dress over her head, dropping it to the floor.

That's when Olivier tackled her so that she fell

back on her bed, his hands on her wrists, his mouth on her neck. Her back arched as pure dragon fire ran through her veins.

"Oh," she moaned.

Not to be outdone, Gahariet pushed his brother aside a little.

"I want to feast, too." She felt her thighs being pushed apart. Gahariet's hair was rubbing against her inner thigh.

Then his tongue was touching her core. "Mmm, you're so wet." He licked her from top to bottom, paying special attention to her clit every time that he got up there.

She bucked wildly, but his hands went to her hips to hold her still as he ate his fill of her.

Olivier stopped kissing her and moved up her body, his knees going on either side of her shoulders.

"Open up, mate," Oliver told her. He gripped her chin in his hand before guiding his cock into her open mouth with his other.

He tasted so good, so salty, but he was also way too big for her mouth.

"Breathe," Olivier told her. "Just breathe."

She tried to breathe around his cock, but she felt like she didn't have any room.

Olivier's hands were in her hair now as he slid even deeper into her mouth. Her head was held in place by the mattress and all she could see was Olivier above her.

He began to withdraw, and she thought that he was letting her breathe. But he was soon pushing himself right back into her mouth, filling up every available inch and then some. She sucked on him the best that she could, trying to taste his essence with her tongue, but he kept pulling out.

She got frustrated enough to pull his hips with her hands, pulling him towards her as hard as she could.

"You want more?" Olivier pushed into her as deep as she could go. She felt him touching her throat.

Now his hands were on the mattress. He ground into her mouth again and again. She tasted a shot of precome, and then she felt his seed coming out in several pulses, filling her mouth. She swallowed as much as she could.

And then Olivier was done and pulling out of her mouth. Phuong caught her breath then, her eyes closed from the intensity of giving oral while on the bottom.

"You aren't done yet, my dear." While Olivier had ridden her face, Gahariet had slowly been loving her below.

But now that his brother was off of her, he pulled her thighs even wider.

"Are you ready, darling? Do you want it?"

"Yes," she moaned.

He slid inside of her.

"Perfect fit," Gahariet said. "You're our perfect mate."

"Oh," Phuong said, her head tilted back. "Big."

"So tight," he praised. He pulled her legs over his shoulders as he began to piledrive inside of her body, taking her hard enough to hit the headboard against the wall over and over again.

Phuong felt like she was in a turbulent storm. She couldn't hear or see anything while she was this close to an orgasm. She cried out as her body pulled her over the edge and she free-fell into oblivion.

She was distantly aware that Gahariet was loving her even harder now, until he grunted and spilled himself inside of her body, filling her up.

Then he got off of her. She was still struggling to breathe after her orgasm.

"Do you feel warm?" Olivier asked, as if that had been the main point of their loving. His hand traced over the curve of one soft breast before going down to her waist.

"Very," Phuong told him. She leaned over and bit his shoulder gently. "Thank you."

Gahariet was behind her. He positioned himself so that he was spooning her from behind while Olivier was right in front of Phuong.

"Rest," Gahariet commanded. "You've had a big day, and your body isn't done with the transition."

Phuong could have protested, but she was getting

sleepy after they had gotten wild.

She couldn't stay awake any longer and drifted off.

## Gahariet

Gahariet woke up when somebody knocked on Phuong's door. He looked at the discarded clothing on the floor, which was still wet. He grimaced. He went to Phuong's closet and grabbed her dressing robe. The Draka didn't mind nudity, but their Yore servants sometimes did.

He went and opened the door. "Yes?"

"There's somebody here to see you. She says that she knows you."

"Who?"

"A Yore seer."

Gahariet looked down at himself. He was dressed in a woman's dressing robe.

"I have to go to my room to get some clothes, but I'll be downstairs in five minutes, okay? Just tell her to wait. I want to hear what she has to say."

Gahariet ran into his own room, one hand keeping the dressing robe firmly shut. He threw on some of his loosest clothing before heading downstairs. He didn't look like a prince at the moment, but he didn't care.

When he got downstairs, he stopped and froze.

The Yore seer was the one from the market, the one who had told Olivier about his mate.

Raising one eyebrow, Gahariet said, "To what do we owe the pleasure?"

She didn't answer his question, instead asking her own. "She's come, hasn't she? I can feel her."

Her eyes were slowly turning silver, first around the edges and then in the middle. Gahariet wanted to be careful. She could be one of the Yore who could pull mind tricks. Even if she didn't like the Drakan Thrones, Gahariet knew that she seemed to be emotionally invested in Phuong's well-being. Stars, she'd predicted Phuong's arrival, hadn't she? Gahariet tried to ignore what else she had predicted.

"Why don't you come upstairs with me? We need someone to watch over her, and you might be a good choice. Do you have any references? Any experience?"

"Just watching after my own family, that's all."

"It could be enough. Come."

Gahariet went up the stairs as the Yore seer followed him slowly behind. They could both hear the creaking of her joints.

Gahariet didn't know why, but his instincts said that he could trust her. Something about her made him confident that she wouldn't hurt Phuong.

"It's okay if you don't have any experience. The other personal attendants can bring you up to speed, and it's a unique position anyway. Come see her."

They were at Phuong's door. He abruptly realized that his twin and his mate were naked.

"Hold on. Stay out here for a little while." The Yore sank gracefully and sat on her heels while Gahariet ducked inside of the room.

Phuong was still asleep, but Olivier was awake. He was tracing the edges of her barely visible scales with the tips of his fingers.

"The seer is here."

Olivier turned. "The seer from the market?"

"Yup. Get dressed."

Olivier went to Phuong's closet and chose one of her dresses unabashedly. It was a simple tunic, and it looked unisex. Gahariet wished that he'd had the luxury of choosing whatever he wanted. Olivier looked like the clothing belonged to him, while Gahariet was sure that he'd looked absolutely ridiculous in the pink dressing robe.

"We have to get Phuong dressed, too."

"What?" she asked sleepily. "What's happening?"

"Just put on a dress," Gahariet said. He went to her

wardrobe and grabbed one. He pulled the covers off of her and she yelped.

"Cold!"

"Put on a dress. There's someone waiting outside who wants to meet you very much."

Phuong stilled and stopped trying to pull the covers back. She took the dress that Gahariet offered and shimmied into it. It was purple, indigo, and green with hints of blue in several places.

"Who is it?"

"She's a Yore seer. She foretold that you would come to us. And now that you're here, she wants to meet you."

Phuong looked confused. "She knew that I'd be your mate?"

"Yes." Gahariet could have explained more, but it was a little more complicated than that. "Everybody is fine now, right?"

Phuong and Olivier nodded.

Gahariet went out to the door to bring the Yore seer into the room.

When she got into the room, she immediately got to her knees at the foot of Phuong's bed.

"Are you okay?" Phuong said. "Gahariet, help her up."

"I don't need to be helped up, my queen," the Yore seer said softly. "I am not quite that old."

"Queen? I have no crown, no throne. At best I thought that I was a princess."

"Your parents are gone, my dear. That means that you ascended to the throne. You and your brother are quite close in age, but you're the eldest child. And in Yore culture, it's an absolute monarchy. It doesn't matter that he's a boy. You have the right to the throne."

The dragon twins looked at each other. What she was talking about was pure treason, but they wanted to hear more.

"My family thought that I had finally gone crazy. I saw that a lost Yore royal would mate with two Draka at the seat of royalty. Such an alliance would change the balance into Yore favor. They said that it seemed too far-fetched. But I knew the whole time that my visions never lied. I'm descended from what should have been the royal advisory. If the Yore still ran this world, I would be on your council as a voice of spiritual guidance."

"That's a whole lot to process," Phuong said weakly.

"She's a queen?" Gahariet asked. "But she hasn't had a coronation ceremony."

"The royal children were lost years ago. We've been searching for them for a long time, but the men who killed their parents must have felt merciful towards small children. And now they are full-grown adults. Where is your brother, Phuong?"

"Xuan? He's in hiding."

"Now that you're safe, you can call him out."

"I don't think that's a good idea." Phuong shifted uncomfortably on the bed. "He's not going to be very happy that I mated two Drakan Thrones."

"Nonsense," the seer said. "Perfect nonsense. This is the only way."

"Well, you are hired now," Gahariet said. He liked the seer's style, even though he still didn't know her name. "You can be Phuong's personal attendant." From the smiles on both of their faces, it was a good choice.

## EMPTY BOTTLES

Marc

*M*arc poured the rest of his current bottle of wine into his glass. There were five empty bottles on the table next to him.

Lucien said, "Snap out of it. Whatever happened, it's not worth drinking this much booze. Dragon metabolisms are magical, but not that magical. You can still kill your liver. Honestly, you've been moping around here for too long."

"Not long enough. Not if I can still remember." Marc drained the glass in one gulp.

"If one plan fails, we'll just try something else."

Marc didn't say anything in reply. He could feel Phuong now, just like he felt other Draka. The twins had won yet again.

It was unfair that, just by being born, they were always going to be on the winning side.

He heard a boom and his face snapped up to look at his brother, whose fist was on the table. His brother's eyes were flames.

"Finish what you started, Marc. There are enough of us to take down two baby royals who don't even wear their crowns."

Marc stood, not too steadily. "I don't like your tone, Lucien."

His brother put his hand in the center of Marc's chest and forced him to sit down again.

"Get off of me." Marc knew that his eyes had burst into flames.

"Look at you," Lucien sneered. "The head of the wealthiest auction house on Vestra and it doesn't mean anything at all. Our mother would be ashamed."

Marc tried to stomp on Lucien's toe, but somehow it felt like he was doing it in slow motion. He'd had a lot of alcohol.

"Sleep it off, brother," Lucien said as he stepped away from Marc's attempts to hit him. "Tomorrow, we'll make a plan."

QUESTIONS

Phuong

Phuong felt much better than she had felt the day before. She felt more like herself. After Gahariet had brought food up from the kitchens for the four of them, she got started on a barrage of questions.

"Did you know my parents?"

"In passing, not very well, my dear." The seer turned and looked at her mates. Phuong got the impression that even if she did know a lot about the dead royals, she wouldn't say it in a room with two Draka. That was a shame. Then Phuong realized that she didn't even know her new attendant's name.

"What's your name? You already know mine, which means that you knew about me."

"My name is Hoa. Yes, we did know about you, but Phuong is a common name, so we couldn't find you by asking about little girls named Phuong. That could've gotten you killed. Your parents named you Phoenix because they knew that you would bring the Yore back to greatness."

Phuong shook her head. "I can't bring the Yore back to greatness. I'm just an orphan."

"You're our queen," Hoa said simply. "You must. It is your destiny."

Phuong felt the burden of her responsibility to her people settle like a physical weight on her shoulders.

She didn't know how to be a queen. She didn't even know how to be a princess.

## NEW BEGINNINGS

### Gahariet

Gahariet had noticed that the seer, Hoa, had looked at him and his brother before cautiously answering some of Phuong's questions. Phuong was full of a million questions, but Gahariet wasn't paying that much attention. He looked instead at Hoa's body language. She'd been deferential, a Yore in a Draka castle, but now that she was with a woman that she called queen, her whole posture was different. Yes, she was kneeling on the ground, but her face was full of light and hope.

Interesting.

Could Phuong really be the girl that they were looking for? Time would tell, he supposed.

Hoa was careful enough to make Gahariet feel good about keeping her close to Phuong. Her cautiousness made Gahariet feel like she was safe and unlikely to be paid by Marc to lure Phuong back into his arms. Marc had quite a bit of money, which talked eloquently, especially when the Yore had very little.

Phuong was their mate now. Nothing could break that bond. However, Marc could start a war if he became fixated on their mate. He said that she belonged to him, even though she didn't. Phuong wasn't a spoil of war. She was a precious princess.

The whole time, the four were eating, three of them seated on the bed, the older Yore on her knees on the ground. There were clearly empty chairs in the room, but she didn't move towards any of them.

Gahariet interrupted their intense conversation to say, "You can sit in a chair, you know."

"I don't want to," the seer quickly replied. "This is the proper way to address my queen."

Gahariet shrugged and let it go. Far be it from him to violate royal Yore protocol. He had a feeling that it was nothing like the royal Draka protocol.

When there wasn't any food left, Phuong poured out four glasses of wine from the small bottle that Gahariet had brought upstairs.

"I'd like to propose a toast." Phuong passed out each glass of wine.

"To new beginnings and old revelations."

"Cheers!" The four of them clinked their glasses, Hoa still kneeling on the ground.

"This would be perfect," Phuong said, "if my brother were here." She sighed before turning to look out of her window.

Simultaneously, Olivier and Gahariet looked at each other. They had searched far and wide for her brother. They'd used their normal investigators, but her brother was a ghost. They knew that she knew where he was hiding, but she wasn't telling them. And if they couldn't find her brother, they were going to have to hope that Marc would also be unable to find him.

"Excuse me," Phuong gasped, quickly putting her wineglass down. She jumped out of bed and ran to her bathroom. Gahariet could hear the sounds of her retching into the toilet.

The Yore seer got to her feet and sprinted into the room, holding back Phuong's hair as she emptied the meal that she'd just eaten right back out.

## ACID

### Phuong

Phuong spat the taste of acid out of her mouth. She got to her feet and rinsed.

"I'll go get you some fireweed tea and maybe flatbread. Your stomach can't handle much right now."

Hoa was so obviously concerned about her that Phuong had to admit it was nice for someone to care about her well-being so much.

Hoa ran downstairs and came back up with a pot of tea, a teacup, and flatbread.

"Is she okay?" Gahariet asked Hoa. "She's drunk

our blood, so she's turning into a dragon, but I don't think that it's normal to vomit during the process."

"Her vomit has nothing to do with transitioning into being a dragon."

"Tell me what it means, then." Phuong crossed her arms. "What are you talking about?"

Hoa looked straight at Phuong's lower stomach.

"I can sense the children inside of you. You're having twins."

PHUONG ROLLED over for the eighth time that night, but she just couldn't get comfortable. "You're having twins." Hoa's words echoed in her mind over and over again.

Being pregnant with baby dragons was an overwhelming prospect, but she knew that she already loved the children who were growing inside of her. She still missed her brother, and Marc still had it out for her. But her dragon mates were protective, and she knew that the overprotectiveness would escalate while she had babies.

She'd asked to sleep alone tonight, which meant that she was alone in her cold room. She walked to the window.

Hearing something, she turned her head. Her hearing was sharpening. She saw a flicker of shadow in the corner of her eye, then she heard what sounded like an army of flapping wings in the air.

## ANOTHER ATTACK

Olivier

*O*livier rubbed his eyes. It was late at night, and the Assembly inquiries were just too boring. He wasn't in the mood to deal with all of them.

"Do you hear that?" Gahariet asked.

Olivier listened hard. "Wings." His eyes turned to flame.

Olivier threw open the window before dissolving into smoke. Gahariet followed him up to the highest tower in their castle.

"I knew that he'd be back."

"He has reinforcements."

Jumping out of the tower, they shifted into their dragon forms as they fell. Then they chased the winged meddlers off, one by one. They were in a ring around the castle, and it was easy for the brothers to chase them off. Their flames blew hot as they overwhelmed the attacking party. Their dragons, royal dragons, were much larger than the average Draka. It was crazy for anybody to attack a Draka castle, especially a royal one. The attackers would soon find that out.

It was a very confusing and suicidal attack, but they soon had slaughtered all of the small Lockwings who had been sent to them.

They flowed back to Phuong's room. She had left her bedroom window open a crack. They would have to tell her to try to be safer.

Hoa was at Phuong's bedside, weaving together some sort of mat.

"Your Highnesses," she said. Olivier wondered if she was going to sink to her knees, but apparently Draka weren't going to be treated like a Yore royal.

She set the mat aside. "Are you hurt? Do you need any kind of help?"

"Don't worry. It was just Lockwings. They're a minor threat, and honestly, they're an insult more than anything."

Hoa nodded at them, digesting their words for a moment, before she said, "You're right, the Lockwings don't matter. I need to tell you more about the prophecy."

"We're listening." Olivier sat on the bed and stroked Phuong's light silver hair with one hand. She smiled in her sleep.

"I'm sure of what I saw. Your children — the dragon babies born to a Yore queen — are destined to change this entire world when they are kings. They will be dragons in spirit more than they will ever be Yore, and the Yore will rebel against it."

Gahariet raised one eyebrow, but Olivier was still listening intently.

"How do you know the gender..."

Hoa's eyes were glowing silver now. "The babies must make it into the world before they can become kings, and there will be a number of attempts to ensure that they don't."

Olivier caught his brother's eyes. Olivier knew that Gahariet didn't put much faith in Yore predictions, but Olivier thought that her prophecy was pretty much common sense. Yes, there were plenty of Yore-Draka pairings...but as far as he knew, they were the only Thrones to take Yore wives. With the quantity of Draka and off-world girls thrown at them, most Draka princes didn't need to marry Yore.

Gahariet and Olivier had mated Phuong purely by choice and a little bit of luck.

If the seer was right, the children who were growing inside of Phuong would be little boys.

Olivier smiled at the thought of chubby little dragonlings running around the castle. It would be fun to teach them how to fly.

"I must go to bed," Hoa told them, rising from her chair in the corner. "But think about what I said to you. The threat is very real. If they aren't born, then this world will stay just as it is."

With that, Hoa walked out of the room.

"I understand why that's bad for the Yore, but what do we have invested in it? We're Drakan Thrones...we rule this planet." Olivier turned to his brother. "So why would we care?"

"We care because those twins are our children, Olivier." Gahariet sighed. "We will protect them until they are born, and we'll protect them beyond that. We have the money and the fighters to do it. I just hope that Phuong has a healthy pregnancy. We can fight Marc, but we can't fight sickness. Pregnancy is a fragile time."

Olivier stared at Phuong, who was all the way under the sheets. Nobody could even see that she was pregnant yet, although Phuong's scent had definitely changed.

It would be months before she had the babies. They'd just have to stay close.

## BLAST

Phuong

*P*huong's eyes shot wide open. She looked down at her hand and saw that her new dragon scales were close to the surface of her skin and glowing.

What had woken her up? She closed her eyes again and concentrated. She could feel Marc. He was very close. She could feel his evil intent like a cold wind wrapping around her, trying to pull her away from the castle.

She jumped out of bed. Apparently her dragon mind and Yore blood could pierce beyond just getting faint impressions from him.

He wanted to attack her. She knew that. He wasn't here to persuade her to leave.

She got out of bed and went straight out into the hallway. She looked in Gahariet's and Olivier's rooms, but they weren't there.

She went downstairs and looked in the dining room and the kitchen, but they weren't there either.

Finally, she found them in the library.

"What are you two doing in here?"

"Researching," Gahariet replied. "Is everything okay?"

She looked at them. Why wouldn't they tell her what was going on?

Right then, an enormous blast struck the castle.

"Stay here," Gahariet told Phuong. She frowned, but she stayed still as he and his brother went out.

One minute later, she followed them out the door. She wanted to see what was going on. She slowly climbed to the top of one of the towers.

From up there, she could see the twin dragons defending their stronghold against Marc's brood, who had encircled them. Dragons were a lot more dangerous than Lockwings. Their eyes were flames.

Phuong knelt and tried to hide while still being able to see. They wanted to come for her. All of this trouble was for her.

The castle shook as Gahariet slammed two other dragons into the walls. Her mates were absolutely marvelous. There was an enormous number of dragons set against them, but they didn't seem to be intimidated by the odds.

They fought the intruders, dodging in and out. For such huge creatures, they were incredibly graceful.

Her dragon mind wanted to help them defend their home, but that same primal mind knew that she had to keep the children safe.

The eyes of all the dragons glowed, their fires burning hotter and hotter.

Suddenly, there was a turning point in the battle. The attack brood began to wing backward, away from her mates. Her heart was thumping hard in her chest.

"My queen."

Phuong spun around to see that Hoa was behind her. Phuong could see that she was crying, so she pulled Hoa into a hug and pulled her down the steps of the tower.

As they got to the ground floor, she could see wisps of smoke that solidified into her mates.

"Are you okay?"

"No time for that," Gahariet said briskly. "We have to search the lower levels to make sure that they're really gone. The aerial attack could have been a distraction."

Gahariet and Olivier turned around and left Phuong with Hoa.

## Gahariet

An hour later, the twins had checked every nook and cranny underneath their castle. Nobody was there, not even the Yore servants.

Gahariet's body suddenly felt like he needed about 10 years of sleep. Adrenaline could do that.

He slumped and sat on a box, his brother settling beside him.

"That took a lot out of me," Olivier admitted. "I think that we need to train more."

"I agree," Gahariet said. "We won, but it wasn't all that easy. I feel so sore." He flexed his shoulders.

"He was bolder than he's ever dared to be."

"We could fix it," Olivier said. "All we have to do is say that she's carrying our child. No court would ever let him keep her."

"I think that it wasn't Marc behind this one."

"What are you talking about? It was Marc's brood, wasn't it?"

"It was Lucien, I just know it," Gahariet said. "He was here. He is trying to use Marc's fixation against him. They're probably going to try to take our place."

"They aren't royal, and they certainly aren't dragon enough to take our crowns from us."

"But he is cunning. We need to keep an eye on the situation."

Gahariet and Olivier went to Phuong's room. They heard the sounds of her vomiting in the bathroom again.

"Is she okay?" Olivier asked. "She's gone through a lot lately."

Hoa turned and met their eyes. "You need to be

quick. She needs to see a healer. Whatever this is, it isn't natural."

"What about the babies?"

"I think that whomever is attacking her doesn't know about the babies, but I don't know what's going to happen when the attacker discovers that she is pregnant."

"We have the best healers in the area. We'll take her down to the medical bay."

* * *

THEY HAD a healer who was well versed in both Draka and Yore medicine, a necessity when the household was so large.

He ran a few tests on Phuong before talking to them.

"Nothing seems to be amiss. It wasn't meant to hurt her."

"What possible reason could there be for making her feel like this?" Olivier asked.

"I don't know," the healer admitted.

"Maybe Marc wants to draw her out. He keeps attacking our castle and failing."

"I could do something to help."

"Oh?" Gahariet looked at the healer, who looked uncomfortable.

"I can detach her from her blood, but it's not really...legal."

"We're princes," Olivier said. "What's the point of being a Throne if you can't take risks?"

"We set an example for everyone else, Olivier. You know that."

"What could be better than keeping our mate safe? Is that something that we should be ashamed of?"

"We're in," Gahariet said grimly. "Do what you need to do to take care of her."

"It'll take some time," the healer warned. "And it won't keep him away forever. It's temporary."

"Do it," Olivier said, flames leaking into his eyes. "I'll stay here for as long as I need to."

The healer nodded and began to rummage around in a cabinet.

"Excuse me," Gahariet said before he walked out of the room.

His heart was heavy as he left. Could he fight something that was invisible? He and Olivier would do everything they could, but could they prevent her own blood from turning against her?

They would have heirs soon, but his dragon was restless when it came to protecting the children. He knew that Marc might be pretty unethical, but he wouldn't harm children. Lucien was another matter.

"Hello, prince."

Gahariet spun around to see a young Yore man standing behind him. He lowered his center of gravity just a little bit and adjusted his stance. He might be paranoid, but after the Lockwing attack, anything could happen.

He could feel his eyes start to heat, ready to begin flaming.

"There are rumors that you took in a girl. Very pretty? Answers to Phuong?"

"Why are you asking?"

"She's my sister."

# FOUND

Phuong

**P**huong could hear people talking around her in the medical bay, speaking in low whispers. She wasn't sick, but the procedure had been pretty exhausting. The doctor had taken all of the blood out of her body, cleansed it, and put it back in. It had been cold when it went back in, and now she felt like she was an ice cube.

"Phuong?"

Was she dreaming? That voice sounded just like Xuan. She opened her eyes to see the familiar twinkle of her brother's eyes.

She felt a wave of warm relief wash over her. She

sat up. He came in for a quick hug, but she held onto him for a little longer than was strictly necessary.

When she let go, she said, "How did you find me?"

Xuan just grinned down at her. "I have ears. I've been looking for you, and I heard a rumor that you were here."

"I meant to come to you. I tried to…"

"Don't worry about it, Phuong."

He looked at Olivier and Gahariet, who were watching the family reunion.

"I can see that you're mated."

"And there's something else you should know."

"Yeah."

Phuong put her hand on her stomach.

"I need to tell you something."

"Are you sick?" He looked around the medical bay. "Is there something wrong?"

"A little sick," Phuong admitted, "but I have great news. I'm having a baby. Well, two."

Xuan hugged her fiercely this time. "There won't be a more perfect mother on this entire planet. I can't wait to meet your kids." He kissed his sister's cheek. "Wow!"

# PART III

## RECLAIM

### Phuong

"his reunion is great, but we have to reclaim your blood from Marc."

Phuong leaned back in her bed, all the joy drained out of the moment by the reality check. They didn't have to clarify what they meant. She knew that they were right. She looked back at her brother.

Gahariet continued, in his deep voice, "It will mean invading their territory."

Phuong's stomach dropped. Gahariet wanted them to storm the auction house, which was their stronghold. She couldn't think of anything worse. Her hand went to her stomach.

"The babies will be safe. If push comes to shove, we'll say that you're pregnant. Marc would never hurt any child, Draka or Yore."

Her brother grabbed some red chom chom from a bowl on Phuong's nightstand. He ate it.

"I like it. I would like to repay Marc for the trouble he's caused."

Phuong knew that Xuan was angry about Marc trapping Phuong when they had robbed the auction house, but Xuan also had his underground reputation to protect. Marc and Xuan moved in a small sea full of sharks; showing weakness meant that you were food. He needed to figure out a way to reestablish his credibility.

It was a macho thing.

"We could just stay here, where we're safe," Phuong suggested.

"Or we can protect our family." The three boys spoke in unison.

Phuong winced. They'd obviously made up their minds.

## GOADING

### Marc

"**You** botched the perfect time to snatch her. You're losing your touch, brother."

Marc didn't say anything, but his fists were clenched.

"You pulled back when you should've pushed forward. You were already inside of her mind...and now what do you have? You're changing her body a little bit? That's ridiculous. We should've taken her when she was in the medical bay."

Marc still didn't respond. There was something slightly strange about Phuong. There was something in her aura that felt different. She was much bigger in spirit now.

Yes, of course some of the change was due to taking dragon blood. But there was more than that.

"Maybe we should try to..."

Marc stopped listening to his brother, but he nodded at appropriate intervals. Lucien hated the twins even more than he did. As the oldest, Lucien had spent his young years in a very poor Draka family, before their father had dug them out. Yes, they were part of generations of criminals, but their grandfather hadn't been especially great at what he did.

"And then we can be Thrones," Lucien finished. "What do you think?"

"I need more time to think about it." Marc got to his feet and walked out of the room.

# SPELLBOOK

## Phuong

*P*huong looked at Hoa.

"Wow. This book is huge and old."

"It has all the old Yore spells and rituals that can bring you up to speed on what a queen should do. Your parents entrusted the Yore to give it to you when you were of age and able to use it. Now it's your time."

For her whole life, Phuong's identity had been a mystery. Yes, she knew that she was Yore. She could see that in the mirror. But she had no idea about Yore magic.

She couldn't read the spell book all that well, but she had Hoa with her. The characters in the book weren't anything like the Standard characters that the Draka used. And even though she had a little Draka blood in her now, her Yore heritage was the strongest call.

"What should I memorize first?" Phuong felt overwhelmed by the foreign characters. She felt like she was a little child learning how to read all over again. There was a part of her that felt as if she should've learned Yore characters earlier than the Draka ones...but she'd been in an orphanage, a lost princess.

"You need to internalize the magic that you have, not memorize some spells. These spells are just the basics. As you use magic more and more, you'll be able to do more. We're going to train you in basics first."

"If the Yore have magic, why were the Draka able to take over?"

Hoa sighed. "The Yore thought that the Draka were just merchants. We welcomed them on our planet, no matter how many people they wanted to bring. It was a fatal mistake. Once they had enough people and technology on the planet to take over, they did. Your parents went into hiding before being found and murdered. Most Draka don't know that you and your brother even exist, or you would've been killed as children."

"So Yore magic isn't that powerful?"

"It depends on what you consider powerful. A small amount of power in the right place can help. Think about the first rock that falls during a rock slide. You can do that."

"I can start rock slides?"

"Or avalanches. A very small amount of magic in the right place can help you."

"But the Yore didn't use it before."

"That's because when you use the power of nature, you're blasting innocent people, too. It wasn't as if the Yore rulers were going to murder thousands of their own people in order to beat back a few hundred Draka. We thought that we would prevail until we couldn't."

"How do you know all this?"

"It's Yore history."

Phuong hadn't learned any Yore history in school. She'd learned all about Draka conquests and their space exploration attempts, but she realized that she knew nothing of her own history.

"So how fast can I learn how to do this?"

"Maybe in four years, you'll be able to light a candle."

Phuong was angry. "That's not going to help my mates now."

Phuong began to flip through the pages. They were all covered with hand-drawn artwork and characters.

"What's this one?" She could see someone with silver eyes staring at someone whose eyes reflected the silver.

"It's a mind link."

"What supplies do we need for it?"

"It just takes incense and powerful focus. But that's definitely not where you should start."

"I appreciate your caution, but I want to do it. There's no time for me to waste dallying around with basics. If Marc uses my blood again and overwhelms my spirit, I want to be able to fight back."

## RAINING KISSES

Olivier

livier and Gahariet went to check in on their mate. "You look exhausted," Gahariet said. "You did too much today."

"I'll survive," Phuong said, smiling even though she looked totally wiped out. She was a little pale.

Hoa was there in the corner. "Excuse me, Your Highnesses. I need to go home. I need to watch my granddaughter."

She bowed with her arms crossed to the three royals. Maybe Hoa was growing to like them.

Olivier crossed the room to pull Phuong into his

arms as soon as Hoa was gone. He pulled her hair, wrapping it around his hand as he pulled her backwards, raining kisses on her forehead, eyes, cheeks, nose, and finally mouth. Then he kissed and bit her neck. She smelled like flowers and pastries.

"Did you bake something today? We have people for that."

"Well, we had to find incense, but the only incense that we could find was vanilla-scented. Hoa said that it might interfere with my concentration, but we had to use it."

"That's why you smell so nice." He licked her neck. "Mmm."

"Save some for me," Gahariet admonished. He was taking off his shirt and pants and carelessly leaving them on the floor. He came around Phuong's other side, sliding his hands around her and wrapping her in his arms. His chin came down on the top of her head.

Phuong shivered a little.

"Are you cold?" Olivier cupped one of her breasts and felt that one of her nipples was hard.

"No," she whispered. She tilted her head, moving Gahariet off of her, while Oliver kissed her mouth.

"There's no bed in the study," she said when she broke the kiss.

"We can improvise."

Gahariet leaned down to grasp the hem of Phuong's dress. It was ocean blue with navy blue straps at the top, with two cut-outs showing just a tiny bit of the tops of her breasts. Olivier leaned down to taste her skin there.

"You taste good all over."

Then Gahariet was pulling the dress over Phuong's head. He picked her up and pulled her away from Olivier, bending her over the desk. Her feet were on the ground. Gahariet's hand was in her hair.

"Widen your stance," he told her.

Olivier watched as Phuong spread her legs a little wider. Gahariet's hand began to rub her lower lips.

Olivier walked to Phuong's front and rubbed his precome on her mouth.

"Mmm," she said, licking her lips before taking his cock into her mouth.

Olivier batted away Gahariet's hands so that he could control Phuong's head as she gave him the blowjob of his life. His eyes were closed. The only thing he could feel was her warm, wet mouth on him.

Phuong was moving back and forth in a steady rhythm. Olivier could hear Gahariet's skin slapping against Phuong's as his brother took her beautiful body over and over again.

Then Olivier's body was exploding into a million points of light. His breath came in big gasps as he released inside of her talented mouth.

"Stars," he said when he could talk again. He found a nearby chair and flopped down into it.

He watched Gahariet continue to take her body. Now that he was sitting down, he could watch Phuong's face as his brother took her small body again and again. At this point, she was pushed up on her tiptoes, and even then, she wasn't touching the ground all the time. On the upstroke, his brother was pushing their mate off of the ground and pulling her back as he withdrew.

Her mouth was open in a perfect O. He could see her tongue, and it made him begin to get hard again. He'd never get enough of her.

Gahariet's hand went to grab a chunk of her hair again.

"Come," Gahariet commanded Phuong.

Phuong's legs were shaking.

"Ah!" she said as Gahariet slammed into her hard enough to move the table, which was solid oak.

Gahariet leaned down and bit her shoulder hard.

Phuong screamed as she went over the edge.

Then Gahariet's hand was wrapping around Phuong's throat, slamming her backwards onto his body.

"That's right, yes," he groaned. Gahariet's eyes closed, and Olivier knew that his brother was coming inside of their mate.

Then Gahariet and Phuong were done.

"I had no idea that I had any strength left after today, but you definitely proved me wrong."

"We can give you our strength this way, as much as you need while you condition your senses and stretch your limits."

"You can give me strength through sex? That's some information that seems very self-serving."

"No, it's true. How do you feel now?"

Phuong stretched a little. "Content and happy."

"How does your body feel?"

She lay there on the table a little longer.

"Much better than it did before we had sex," she said.

"Your scales are more defined now." Olivier snapped to look. Gahariet had taken a much closer look at their mate around the end. Olivier was able to get to his feet now, so he went to the table and inspected their mate's skin.

It was true. She had the scales of a dragon all over

her. They were glowing quite brightly, brightly enough that he wondered how he hadn't noticed. Brightly glowing scales weren't usual for the Draka.

"You're become more of a dragon every day." Olivier leaned in and kissed her fast and hard, not passionately but aggressively all the same. "I can't wait to meet our children."

Phuong's smile was one of the most gorgeous things that Olivier had ever seen.

"I can't wait either." She reached for Olivier's hand and squeezed it.

## NET

### Phuong

*P*huong sat down by the lagoon with the spellbook. She felt confined inside of the castle, no matter how luxurious it was.

She flipped through the Yore magic book. Hoa had taught her the basic characters, but she wasn't all that great at reading Yore yet. She could try, though.

She whispered the words of the spell before she closed her eyes and wiped away everything else, all of her worries, her cares.

Her energy was better than it had been in the

morning the previous day. Whatever the twins had done to her body, it made her stronger.

With her eyes closed, she could feel the life force of several small animals in and around the lagoon. She'd never felt more alive than when she was reaching out and touching all these little sparks. She loved the surge of force that she suddenly had, now that she'd mated with her mates to renew her energy.

But then something went wrong. When she spread the net around herself, she must've opened a door, because she could feel Marc coming in.

She tried to open her eyes and shake herself out of her light trance, but he didn't let her. His taste in her mind made her stomach churn. This time, it was different.. He didn't waste time trying to convince her that she belonged to him.

His essence began to take over her mind.

"Don't be afraid."

It only made her more afraid. She tried to shake him out of her mind, without any clue of how to do that. She didn't know how to successfully repel a mind attack.

She was a queen. A queen should be able to push him out. She thought about blank whiteness in an attempt to shield her real thoughts from him. She didn't want him to learn about her plans.

"I don't mean you any harm, but there are other people who would be only too happy to use you. You are mine, claimed by me, but I will leave the choice to you. Visit your ancestors in these waters. Learn what they want you to learn. Ask them where you belong, if they do not send you straight to me, I will leave you alone. You can live for the rest of your life with the twin princes."

Phuong didn't say anything.

Then his presence was out of her mind. She hadn't reacted in time to tell him that she was definitely not his to claim.

She wouldn't tell anybody about it. After all, her Yore ancestors had told her to be wary. It wasn't as if they would suddenly change their minds.

She thought guiltily that she should tell somebody

that she was going to the ocean, but she walked by herself to the open ocean. The beach was part of the royal estate, so it was empty.

With her clothing still on, she walked straight into the ocean. The twins had little regard for their clothing, so she got the feeling that she didn't need to be especially careful. They were rich enough to replace anything that they liked.

The ocean closed over her, holding her like a mother. She closed her eyes and sank straight into a light trance, opening her mind to the ancestors who still roamed in the ocean water.

She began to feel the spirits of the ancient Yore reaching towards her.

"Guard your throne," one said.

"Guard your throne, a second spirit said.

Then it was a chant as the whole ocean filled with spirits telling her to guard her throne.

Phuong's eyes snapped open as she awoke from her trance. Guard her throne? What did that mean?

Phuong walked slowly back to the castle, trying to

fit together all the puzzle pieces. She was feeling overwhelmed. The spirits only had three words to tell her. It was totally unclear which direction she should be going in. They hadn't said a word about Marc, but she didn't know if they knew about him. She didn't know which throne they were talking about: the Draka one that she got by marriage or the Yore throne that was hers by birth? How was she supposed to guard and from whom?

She was in her wet clothes, so she went upstairs and changed into something dry. She went back downstairs to grab something from the kitchen, picking up some fresh fruit before deciding to go out to the stables that they kept.

There were horses in there. Phuong shared a little bit of fruit with one that seemed especially bold. "You're pretty, yes you are."

"There you are," Olivier said. He walked into the barn and swept her into his arms. She wiggled out of his hold.

"Are you okay? Are you feeling all right? How are the babies?"

"The babies are fine," Phuong said. "I've got to go."

# SHOPPING TRIP

## Olivier

Olivier turned to Gahariet after Phuong basically ran away from them.

"What just happened?"

"She's worrying about something," Gahariet said.

"Do you think it's about our dad and the Yore king? Did she find out that he helped to speed up the Yore king's decline?"

"We shouldn't tell her. It's ancient history. Most Yore believe we wouldn't be in power if we'd had more mercy."

Olivier was quiet for a moment before saying, "She's different."

"She's ours. She'll be fine. Just give her some time."

The two of them fell into silence as they walked back to the castle.

\* \* \*

PHUONG WAS FINALLY WELL. A week after the meeting in the barn, she was basically a new woman. Even though she was healthy and even more powerful, she wasn't talking much.

She was pushing Olivier and Gahariet away emotionally, and Olivier didn't like it at all.

Oh, sure, sexually, she was wilder than ever. The three of them slept in the same bed every night.

But instead of accepting their energy and sending hers to them, she was draining them. Olivier couldn't help but wonder if she meant to store the energy somehow.

Olivier was walking down stairs when he saw

Xuan sitting on a chair near the door. He was alone.

"Where's Phuong?"

"She went shopping."

"Alone?"

"Yeah. She can take care of herself."

"She's pregnant."

"So?" Xuan asked. "She's fine."

Olivier bit back a curse. He didn't want to get into a fight with his mate's brother, especially since they were close.

"I have to find her."

"Be my guest."

Olivier went running for the levi-car to go to the market.

Olivier got out of the car and ran around the market district to find her, his heart pounding hard in his chest. He was afraid for her. When she was alone, she could be snatched by just anybody.

Finally, he found her in a boutique with more bags than she could carry. There were Yore store attendants who were helping her carry her bags out.

"Oh, good. You can help."

Olivier was suddenly holding as many bags as he could carry.

"What are you doing?"

Phuong was signing something.

"What's that?"

"It's something that authorizes a charge on the royal accounts."

Olivier's eyebrows went straight up. Their father didn't let them sign things straight out of the royal treasury. They had their own personal spending accounts. With their mating so new, they had neglected to set up proper accounts for their mate.

In fact, she hadn't even met their father. Granted, their father wasn't a huge presence in their lives, but it was probably the right thing to do.

"Put them in the levi-car," Olivier sighed. "It's right at the end of the street."

He watched as the Yore with all of Phuong's bags walked to the end of the street.

He stepped in front of her when she walked in the same direction. Olivier grabbed her hand, no easy task with all the bags he was carrying.

"What is wrong? Why did you go out alone?"

"You two are keeping something from me. You aren't telling me everything. I realized that everything I owned was chosen by you or your servants. I want to wear clothing that I get to choose."

"You can wear whatever clothing you want."

"I don't need your permission. I'm supposed to be a queen, but you have been keeping me in the castle."

"To keep you safe."

"I am a queen, not a coward."

"We'll help you, I promise. We know that you have

a big destiny, but we want you to be safe. We have to get your blood back before we'll feel safe."

"I don't want to wait. Marc is only a blip. I barely know who I am. But I'm going to gather all the pieces and put them together, no matter what the price. I will protect the throne that my ancestors want me to guard."

"What are you talking about? Did you have another dream? Phuong, you know that dreams aren't that reliable."

"It wasn't a dream," she protested. "It was a trance."

Olivier looked at her. "Why didn't you tell us about it?"

"I wanted to go through it on my own."

"We're here for you. We're your mates, remember?"

"I know," she said, but Olivier didn't think that she really believed it.

## OFFERING TO HELP

### Phuong

*P*huong put her hands on her pounding temples. She knew that she shouldn't be eavesdropping, but it was clear that the twins were going to fast track their plan. She was barely able to read the Yore characters still, let alone actually use them. After Marc's secret meeting with her in her head, she doubted that they would have too much trouble when they went in and demanded her blood.

But Olivier and Gahariet didn't know about that meeting, and she would be there to help them if she could and prevent things from spiraling out of control. Nobody wanted to go to war over a vial of her blood.

She worried about the other people to whom Marc had referred when he'd spoken to her. When they went to the auction house, they'd be going to a seat of black market power. Stars only knew what Marc had down there. She didn't really want to find out. The pit had been a surprise, and she knew that she and Xuan, even with their careful research, had overlooked some of the defenses.

She knocked on the door, not wanting to eavesdrop anymore.

"Who is it?"

"Phuong."

"Come on in," Gahariet called.

She walked into the study.

"Phuong, we were thinking about fast tracking the plan. How would you feel about that?"

Phuong felt just a little bit relieved. She hadn't realized that she'd been stressed out by the prospect that her mates would keep their plans from her.

"I'm ready for it."

"Are you sure?" Olivier asked. "You can stay home if you want."

"I'm more ready than I've ever been."

Olivier was frowning at her.

She said it even more confidently, "I'm ready to help."

She was sick of the secrets that swirled around her. She knew just a little bit about herself, but it just increased her appetite. She wanted to know everything about who and what she was. And she had a feeling that something would happen in a confrontation with Marc that would teach her something new.

Why had she been thrown aside, if she was the royal heir?

## NEW FLOWERS

### Phuong

The next morning, Phuong looked up as Xuan swept into the breakfast room. He looked straight at her, cool as a cucumber.

But she could see the tension in his shoulders. He had some kind of news.

"Do you want to go up to my room to see the new flowers that they gave me?"

Xuan nodded.

"Excuse us," Phuong said to her mates, who were still stuffing their faces with food. "We'll be down in a while."

Phuong brought Xuan up to her room.

"What is it?" she asked him, knowing something must be troubling him.

"I've learned what we are."

"Gahariet and Olivier know that I'm a royal, and so are you."

"But they didn't tell us that our father wasn't just a king."

Phuong stared at her brother. "What are you talking about?"

"Our father wasn't a lesser king of the Yore. He was the emperor."

Phuong felt her knees wobble. She leaned quickly against the wall. "What are you talking about?"

"The Kiyin stone that was found with us. Your stone spoke to me in my dreams last night. I spent yesterday asking around the Yore. The few who were brave enough to tell me told me that the Kiyin stone isn't royal. It's imperial."

"Why didn't Hoa tell me?"

"She probably didn't want to overwhelm you. It was a shock to find out that you were a queen, let alone an empress."

Phuong pinched the bridge of her nose.

"What does the Kiyin stone do?"

"It has the blood of emperors in its heart."

"What does it do?" Phuong repeated.

"It can help you master your powers."

"You brought it with you when you came to find me?"

"Yeah. That's how it was able to reach me in my dreams. Let's go to my room."

Phuong followed her brother to his room. In his bag, he had the Kiyin stone that they'd been found with outside of Heritage House.

"How could nobody tell us about who we were?"

"It put us at risk," Xuan said. "But watch."

Xuan closed his eyes and spread his fingers out with his open palm facing his bag, the Kiyin stone grasped in his other hand.

Phuong gasped as she saw the bag levitate.

"You have telekinesis?"

"We have telekinesis."

Phuong reached out her hand and tried to levitate the flower that was resting on Xuan's dresser, but she couldn't move it.

"You have to hold the Kiyin stone, Sister."

Phuong held out her hand. Xuan gave her the stone. This time, when she willed the flower to rise, she was shocked to see it begin to float in the air. She was so surprised that she dropped it on the floor. She bent down to pick it up and put it back into the vase.

"I've barely begun to scratch the surface of Yore magic. I learn new things about myself every day."

"So am I," Xuan said.

"This should help," Phuong said. "Can I hold onto the stone?"

"It's half yours, half mine. Of course you can hold onto it if you need it."

Phuong hesitated before she told her brother what had been troubling her.

"I got in touch with the Yore ancestor spirits."

"How?"

"I walked into the open ocean."

"I've been in the open ocean hundreds of times. This planet is mostly ocean. I've never heard the Yore ancestors."

"You don't go into trances like I do."

"True. So you heard them when you went into a trance in the ocean?"

"Yes."

"Take someone with you next time. That could be dangerous."

"I will. Do you want to know what they said?"

"What?"

"They said that I have to guard my throne."

"What does that mean?"

"I don't know, but if I'm an empress, then..."

"We really need to get your blood back."

## MISSION PLANNING

### Gahariet

Gahariet and Olivier were with the small group that they were taking into the auction house. They had hired some Yore seers to navigate through the little-known underground tunnels, using some kind of Yore map that Hoa and Phuong had created that glowed in certain places.

Gahariet hoped that by putting Phuong in the leading position, she'd be pleased, but she was still closed off from them. Her dragon blood made her more temperamental, and he didn't like the way that she had closed herself off from the two of them.

"The east tunnel is guarded by beasts that none of us are prepared for," the Yore seer warned. "Even Marc and his brood avoid them. They are wild guard dogs."

"Just dogs? We can subdue them."

"You don't understand. These are genetically modified dogs. They are several times larger than the creatures that you think of when you think of dogs. They've been bred to attack first. Marc stays far away from them."

The Yore seer's eyes grew even brighter as she intone, "But the west tunnel can be navigated if you have a Yore seer with you. It's a labyrinth, but it's not impossible to get through."

"We could just walk in through the front door," Xuan commented. "It would be easier."

Gahariet turned and looked at his brother-in-law.

"That might be a good idea."

PASSION

Olivier

The second that they were done with their strategy meeting, Phuong ran upstairs to her room. Gahariet and Olivier walked in to find their mate totally naked.

Her temper was in full blaze, and she jumped into Olivier's arms before thrusting her tongue into his mouth.

He was initially surprised, but he held her close as she explored his mouth thoroughly. Olivier could hear the clunk of Gahariet's belt hitting the floor.

Then his brother was pulling Phuong out of his

arms to put her down. Olivier got naked, the last one to make it onto the bed.

This time, his brother pulled Phuong onto her side. He was higher up on the bed withOlivier behind their mate.

Olivier felt the soft seam between her legs, pushing them apart. His fingers carefully probed the wetness there before finding her clit and rubbing it.

He could hear her enthusiastically blowing his brother. He was getting plenty hot and bothered, remembering what it felt like to feel her mouth envelop him.

Then he went down to the bottom of the bed to eat her out from behind, separating her thighs and pushing his tongue inside of her. He could hear a muffled yelp, which told him that he was doing his job right.

She shook in front of him, and he knew that she had come all over his tongue, her juices flowing freely. She had seemed innocent when they started, but she had picked up bedroom skills very quickly.

Olivier slid up, replacing his tongue with the head of his cock, pushing inside of her body. He licked the salt of her dark skin. She tasted absolutely delicious. He loved the smooth texture of her skin.

He pushed his cock all the way in and he heard her choke on his brother's cock. She released it and said, "I almost just bit it."

Olivier smiled. "Maybe it's time for us to do something else."

He withdrew from his mate's body, making his erection feel cold.

"Brother, why don't you take her sweet lips? Both of them."

"With pleasure." Gahariet began to kiss Phuong while pushing his own cock, wet with her saliva, inside of her juicy body.

Oliver was covered in her juices. He took the wetness and spread it in and around her ass.

This time, she wasn't nervous and took it like a champ. She was very relaxed and he was able to get into her without any trouble at all.

"That's so good," Gahariet moaned. "Mmm."

Olivier took Phuong's hip in his hand and began to rock inside of her body, alternating with his brother. When one went in, the other went out. The rhythm was endless, eternal, and primal. It felt like the beat of their hearts. There was something different about Phuong tonight. There was something vulnerable inside of her. Olivier tried to reach into her with his mind. For a while now, she'd distanced herself from her mates.

But tonight the walls were down. Olivier felt her mind right there in the bed. Their mating bond was all the way open. She'd kept them shut out for a long time, but Olivier immediately opened himself to her so that he could merge with her fully.

Olivier didn't mind that she'd shut them out. She was entitled to privacy if she wanted it. So long as she was there with them, open or not, and willing to love them, they'd be fine.

He knew that the distance had bothered Gahariet, but not in the same way that it had worried Olivier.

For years, they'd dated many of the eligible females

in the sector. Sometimes, Olivier felt like he had tried each of the noble and royal females on Vestra.

But Phuong was something even better than any other woman. Any fool could see that she had a great destiny, but her path wouldn't be smooth.

## BAD DREAMS

### Phuong

*P*huong twisted in her bed. She was having another dream from the Yore ancestors. It wasn't a nice dream. Not a nice dream at all.

She was watching an older man with Xuan's face dying. A Draka soldier had just cut through him with a laser sword.

She was crying, her heart aching. Something inside of her knew that the man was her father. There was a bunch of soldiers on the ground in a ring around him, all wearing golden armor. They must have been the royal guard. And when they had all fallen, her father had, too.

Her heart ached hard as she saw her father die. As Phuong knelt beside him, she watched the light fade from his eyes.

"I love you," he told her with his last dying breath.

And she stood, totally startled. Had he been able to see her spiritual form? How could her father who had died in the past be speaking to her in a dream so far in the future? How did he know that she was his daughter or that she was there?

The questions confused her enough to wake her up. She opened her eyes. She stared at the ceiling, her cheeks still wet with tears from watching her father fall in battle.

She re-examined the dream that she had just seen. He looked so much like Xuan that he had to be her dad, or their dad, she guessed. She'd been abandoned so young that she couldn't possibly remember him.

And as he lay dying on the battlefield, he'd looked at her and told her that he loved her.

Could he have seen that she would travel back in time to that moment? She didn't know if Yore abilities included the ability to sense spirits.

Then she shook herself. Of course the Yore could sense spirits. After all, hadn't she communed with them in the ocean herself? Her father would've had real training, and of course he was better at everything than she was.

She guessed that it was a blessing of the stars that he'd been able to see his daughter once more before he died. She guessed that he had known that she was his daughter the same way that she had known that he was her father.

She didn't know why the spirits had shown her that moment. She didn't know how it had happened, but she was sure that the vision was real. Her heart ached for her father.

Xuan looked just like him, with the same silver hair that she had. He had multi-colored eyes, just like Xuan did, and a thin nose and the same two-toned full lips that she had. Her heart hurt, since she couldn't remember seeing him.

But he'd told her that he loved her.

She wrapped herself in a robe and went to stand by the window. She was cold, and she didn't know whether she was chilly because of the castle's temperature or the chilling vision.

## STRANGE DREAMS

### Xuan

Xuan snapped out of a deep sleep. His chest went up and down as he panted. He didn't know what his dream meant.

His bed was too soft. Sure, they'd had nice sheets in their den, but the Draka bed itself was just too squishy.

He couldn't remember clearly what had happened, but he thought that they might be in the keep of their enemies.

Bao Dai, their father, had fallen to the Draka. And here they were, with the empress mated to two Drakans, Thrones no less.

The whispers on the street had said that their father had been destroyed when his empress had died from a mysterious alien sickness. He blamed the Draka for bringing it, of course, but there hadn't been anything that anybody could do for her.

* * *

THE NEXT MORNING, Xuan was walking in the royal gardens with his sister before he found the courage to ask the question that haunted him ever since he had his dream.

"How do we know that we can trust your mates?"

Phuong turned around and asked, "You were pulled into the dream, too?"

"You had it, too?" Xuan asked.

"So you think..."

"He's alive?" Xuan couldn't keep the hope from creeping into his voice.

"No," Phuong whispered. "I watched him die."

"He was magical," Xuan protested. He couldn't

recall exactly what happened in the dream, but he knew that his father had better magic than they did.

Phuong walked a little further. Xuan hurried to catch up with her.

"I've tried to feel him," Phuong said softly. "I've tried to reach for his essence, but there's nothing there. There's no way that he's alive."

Xuan took in a slow breath. "Do you trust the Draka that you've taken as mates, Phuong? Do you trust that they aren't our enemies, the ones who defeated the Yore? The ones who dethroned our father and put us in an orphanage with implants?"

"I don't know," Phuong said. She looked at him and walked away.

# WINE

Phuong

*P*huong wrestled with Xuan's question all day. In all honesty, she didn't know if she could blame her mates for the sins of their race — the millions of Yore that they'd slain while they'd taken over the planet.

Her mates themselves hadn't even been involved. At worst, their father would've been involved in the Draka takeover.

After dinner, the three of them went to Phuong's room. Like they'd done before, they got undressed quickly.

Phuong reached for Olivier's body and his mind.

She wanted to know the answer, even though she was afraid that it would be something that she didn't want to know.

If it was true — if their family had dethroned hers — her heart would shatter into a thousand pieces. She knew that she was in love, even though they hadn't been together for too long. She knew that they were blood-bound mates for life.

But she knew that they didn't always tell her everything. She couldn't read their dragon hearts, the shifter part that held the answer that she was seeking.

Olivier shut her out while he kissed her. His tongue was in her mouth as he kissed her slowly and deeply. Could she accept physical but not emotional closeness?

Then the question became academic, because the three of them were tumbling onto the bed.

Gahariet reached for Phuong first, holding her close, his tongue in her mouth.

Olivier was stroking the curve of her waist and then going all the way down to the back of her knees. Normally, she was ticklish there, but today it made her body feel like it was on fire.

Olivier was pulling Phuong's hands above her head now, keeping them out of the way. Gahariet was pulling her thighs apart and pushing his cock between her legs before entering her completely.

Olivier didn't try to take her back door. Instead, he held Phuong in place while Gahariet pounded into her soft, small body, taking her over and over again until she was crying out, shaking between the two of them, and Gahariet was groaning as he released inside of her.

Phuong was twisting, her hands still held in Olivier's hands. She leaned forward to kiss him. He let go of her hands and planted his hands on her butt, rolling so that she was on top of him.

She used her new freedom to guide his cock into her warm, wet opening. Olivier's eyes rolled back in his head as she rode him, setting a fast and steady pace until she felt him fill her with his seed.

All of them were sweaty, panting, and satisfied.

Physically, anyway.

Afterwards, Phuong stared at the ceiling while she listened to the snores of her mates. She was too afraid to ask them outright about their history with her family — the last imperial family of the Yore.

* * *

THE NEXT MORNING, she was awakened when Olivier kissed her mouth.

"Good morning."

The question had been bouncing around in her head all night. It was out before she could stop it.

"What position did your house take when Emperor Bao Dai fell?"

The twins were absolutely still. Olivier leaned back from her.

"Why won't you answer me?" She felt her eyes filling with tears. She was vulnerable, naked in bed with the two of them, and she was terrified by the total silence.

"We were babies, Phuong."

The tears spilled then.

"Where was your father?" she whispered. "Where was he when the merchant Draka stole the Yore imperial family's wealth?"

Olivier looked down at the bed, which still had some marks of last night's passion.

"We're not our father."

They didn't have to spell it out for her. She understood now. She wasn't sure if their father had directly hurt hers, but she knew that their father had stood by while not lifting a finger to help her father. Why else would Olivier say that they weren't like their father, a king of great power and renown, a warrior who had led the Draka in more than one war, according to her history lessons?

She knew that they were right, that it was unfair to blame them for things that had happened when they were babies. They weren't responsible for what had happened on Vestra.

But what about their father? Had they been raised to despise Yore? Were they the right mates as she looked for a way to re-establish the Yore empire?

She knew that she would love them forever, but

right now, it seemed more like a curse than a blessing.

# LEAVING

## Phuong

*P*huong spent the next day getting pretty. Beauty was a kind of shield against feeling like a helpless object. Hoa helped her get ready for the night, where she'd stand by the Thrones' side while they came back to the auction house.

They were going to march in Marc's front door. The action would publicly announce that they were mated, but she was worried about it becoming public before she was really ready.

She hadn't had the opportunity to connect with any Yore beyond Hoa. Now she was going to announce that she was mated to two Thrones and that she was with child, two children who would be twice royal.

Hoa said that they would be legendary kings.

Then it was time. Gahariet came into her room and leaned against the doorframe.

"You look beautiful."

She turned to smile at her mate. He came to her, put his hands on her waist. He leaned down to kiss her, but she pushed on his chest.

"What's wrong?"

"You're going to mess up my makeup."

"You're stunning, Princess Phuong." He slid his hand over the silk that flowed like water over the curves of her body.

"Thank you for this gown."

"Only the best for our mate, princess, and queen."

He was talking about himself and Olivier, but Phuong felt a twinge. She was supposed to be the Yore empress, and he didn't know exactly who her father was, only that he was deposed Yore royalty.

She cleared her throat. "Are you ready to go?"

He offered her his arm. "Let's go downstairs."

Xuan and Olivier were waiting downstairs. Olivier let out a low whistle on her arrival.

He leaned in to whisper in her ear, "I can't wait to get you naked when we come home later."

She blushed.

"Keep it in your pants, Olivier," Xuan joked. "Ew. Let's go."

They had to take the levi-car. Earlier, the twins had approached on wing and landed on the roof. It was probable that Marc would expect them to come the same way.

So they rode over the hills and towards the auction house.

The levi-car ride was extremely quiet, and Phuong knew why. Xuan wasn't all that comfortable with the Thrones. They didn't know each other. She still hadn't met their father.

"This will be a peaceful recovery of goods, Xuan. Don't worry," she said, trying to reassure her brother. She smiled at him, but she didn't think that it had any impact at all.

Gahariet reached for her hand, but she tugged it out of his grip and tucked a strand of hair behind her hair, before looking out the window.

"I don't understand why you didn't want the guards to come with us."

"Perception is everything in our world," Gahariet told him.

Xuan frowned at Gahariet. "In your world, that might be true. In our world, we like to stay in the land of the living. We should have covered every possibility."

"Why are you suddenly so worried?" Olivier cut in, defending their choices. His eyes were fixated on Xuan.

Xuan shut up, but then he started talking again.

"I stole from him before. He might remember."

"Do you think that he really will?"

"Did he see your face?" Gahariet asked.

"No."

"Then there's nothing to worry about." Gahariet readjusted the collar of his suit.

## INFILTRATION

### Phuong

*P*huong felt wildly uncomfortable in the crush of people in the auction house. She was sick with worry. Her mates looked like they were having a good time, but she could see that their shoulders were tense. She could also feel their feelings through their mate bond, which was normally closed. Maybe the mission had made them open it.

If she could feel them, then Marc must be able to do so, as well.

She could feel the unfriendly gazes of the other

Drakans in the auction house, almost like a heavy weight upon her.

Phuong held her head high. She wasn't a servant. She was twice royal, once by blood and twice by mating. Yes, she had mated men that she wasn't too sure about. All this time, they'd known where she came from, and Xuan had had to tell her.

She wondered if they knew she was imperial. They hadn't told her that she was royal right away...they could easily have kept it from her.

She tried to refocus on the mission. She grabbed a glass of wine from a passing server.

Then Marc headed for them and she almost spilled her wine, her anxiety peaking.

Looking closer at him, he was a little shorter and more heavyset than Marc. The man heading in their direction wasn't Marc at all.

He made a beeline for her mates, ignoring her outright before turning and assessing her thoroughly with his eyes. His eyes made her feel greasy, like she needed a bath.

A split second before he came, Olivier told

Phuong, "Stay quiet while Lucien is here. He's Marc's bloodthirsty brother."

"Your new mate is very beautiful. Is she related to Emperor Bao Dai?"

"We don't know," Gahariet said softly, his hand on Olivier's arm to stop him from saying anything.

"She looks just like him." Lucien grinned at her. It wasn't nice at all. "How nice to meet you. Please enjoy the festivities." He nodded at the Thrones before walking off to talk to a group of people huddled around a hunk of jade carved in the form of a dragon king.

He left behind a stench that made Phuong nauseous. His mention of her resemblance to her real father made the mood tense. Phuong still didn't know if they had known, or if one twin had known and the other hadn't. From the looks of it, Gahariet might have known while Olivier had been very surprised by the accusation and about to set it right.

She didn't want to call them out, not right here, not right now. It wasn't the right place or time. She'd talk to them about it later. She hated being kept in the dark.

Olivier took Phuong's hand and pulled her around the auction house, gently guiding her around the little clumps of Draka who turned to glare at her, the only Yore dressed in fancy clothes besides Xuan. The other Yore were all servers here.

Phuong knew that she was safe with Olivier and Gahariet, but that was intellectual. Deep in her gut, she was terrified of being Marc's doll. Marc wouldn't physically assault Thrones, but she didn't think that any of the Draka would shed a tear if Marc suddenly killed her. Gahariet and Olivier would take revenge, of course, but she'd be dead.

But they were in polite society, and appearance was everything to the Draka.

"You could at least look like you're enjoying yourself, Phuong. We are at a party," Olivier nudged her. "I promise we'll only stay as long as we need to."

"I'm not going to pretend to be someone I'm not," she said stiffly. "And if you didn't realize that when you mated me, then you shouldn't have."

"When we mated, neither of us had any idea who you were." Olivier rubbed his face with his hand. "But this isn't the time."

They looked each other in the eyes. Phuong knew that he was really worried about her and their mating. She instinctively wanted to reassure him that everything was just fine, but she knew that it would be a lie.

## MARC'S INVITATION

Phuong

*A* server came up to her, but he wasn't carrying a tray.

"Marc would like to request the pleasure of your company."

His tone wasn't offensive, but it wasn't the tone of a server. She looked at him closely. He was wearing a simple black suit, but the cloth was higher quality than the other servers.

"Sure, why not," she replied. Gahariet and Olivier trailed behind her as they made their way through the crowd towards Marc's office.

Phuong turned around and met Xuan's eyes. He stopped obtrusively following them, hanging back a few steps and moving at a slower pace. With luck, Marc wouldn't realize that they'd brought somebody extra. Yes, her brother was Yore and stuck out, but he was changing his body language right now to say that he was just a humble Yore server. She could hear one of the Draka ladies give him her empty wineglass and ask for a refill, which he did immediately. He'd be just fine on his own at this party. He had excellent instincts.

Then they were in Marc's office. There were three chairs in front of Marc's desk, and they all took a seat.

"Close the door, please."

The Yore who had fetched them bowed to Marc before closing the door. Phuong was half-expecting to hear the click of a lock, but it never came.

"I think I know what you're here for." Marc pulled a chain out from under his shirt.

All three of them sat up straight in their chairs. There was a vial of blood on the chain. Phuong knew that it was her blood.

His eyes swept over the twins before resting on Phuong.

He sighed. "I had such plans."

"They were your plans, not mine."

Marc paused for a second. "Do you know what I found out when I spent a little extra time with your blood this evening?"

Phuong frowned at him. "What?"

"You're the throneless queen of the Yore. You don't have a kingdom." He laughed softly. "It explains how you draw the eye so simply and unintentionally. You make men want you, to serve you, to please you. That's your natural ability. It's your game. You make the rules."

"I'm not playing any games."

"Oh, but you are. Or you wouldn't be carrying the children of the Thrones."

Phuong gasped while Olivier and Gahariet kept their cool.

"You aimed higher on the social ladder than a mere black market auction house owner. I'm fine with it.

We all deserve to get what we want. You would have been...a crown jewel, if you will, but you're more trouble than you're really worth in the long run. I can't wait until people find out what you are. This whole city will explode."

Olivier banged his fist on Marc's desk.

"Give us her blood."

Marc looked at him.

"I'll give it to you if you tell me why you really want it."

Olivier lost it, pouncing over the desk. But Marc was a dragon, too, and he half shifted. Olivier shifted, too, and tried to pull Marc's vial from his neck.

Finally, after a few minutes of struggling, he broke the chain and threw the vial at Gahariet. He fell on top of Marc's body as the two of them crashed to the ground. Olivier was larger than Marc, and soon he had pinned Marc to the ground.

But the scuffle was loud. The door to Marc's office opened, showing an immediately outraged Lucien.

"What's going on here?"

Marc lifted his hand to stop his brother. Lucien pulled Olivier off of Marc.

He wiped blood from the corner of his mouth. His eyes glowed with just a little bit of flame as he said, "Thank you for coming tonight. The price for the treasure that you've gained tonight will cost you in the long run. I hope you're ready to pay the price."

Phuong didn't like the sound of that at all.

# KITCHEN LOVE

## Phuong

*P*huong was lost in thought and quiet as a mouse on the way back to the castle, just like her brother. There wasn't much to say. She was mostly free of Marc now that they had successfully gotten her blood back. But he had said that he would take a huge price.

She knew that he would make trouble when she attempted to resurrect the Yore empire...which had no land at all. She was certain of it.

Marc hadn't fallen in love with her, just simple lust. But he hated the idea of losing her to the twins, and his personality couldn't stand being robbed.

Her mates had respected the distance that she had set, and she wondered if she should push them away even further. She needed to connect with her subjects with Xuan and Hoa by her side. If she could make the right connections, maybe she could do something.

Olivier helped her out of the levi-car, but she pulled her hand out of his as soon as she got on solid ground.

She wasn't going to invite them into her bedroom tonight.

Gahariet came up behind her and gave her the vial of blood that had caused so much trouble.

Olivier said, "I'm going to get clean."

"Me too."

The twins went inside of the castle, leaving Phuong and Xuan outside.

Xuan said, "What are you going to do now?"

"Right now, all I want is some food and maybe rest. Maybe not in that order. I'm pretty tired."

"Well, go to bed."

She sighed. "I will. Good night, Xuan."

"Sleep tight. It's your first night of peace."

She wondered if it really was. She knew that she still had a rocky relationship with her mates, the descendants of the people who had crushed hers.

She made her way up to her bedroom, got rid of her makeup, pulled off her dress, and snuggled under the covers.

\* \* \*

WHEN SHE WOKE UP, there was a moonbeam shining directly on her eyes, which made her cranky.

Her stomach growled and screamed that she needed more food.

She pulled on a dressing robe and went downstairs. Maybe there would be fruit or something that she could eat, even if the kitchen staff was asleep.

She went downstairs and got into the kitchen, but she froze as soon as she was inside.

Gahariet was sitting right there, slowly eating gateau de xocolatl.

She approached cautiously, her shoulders tense. She didn't know how to talk to him, her own mate, and she wanted to eat, but maybe not at the price of an awkward conversation.

"We're not your enemies." Gahariet's voice was husky.

"I never said you were," she snapped. "I've never said that."

"Yet you keep it from us like it's a secret. Don't you understand how hard it is for us? We never anticipated that we'd mate a Yore."

"What? Are we not good enough for you?" Phuong stuck out her chin, ready for a fight.

"We had no idea that we would mate a Yore princess or that we'd come to love you more than life itself. You know that we're ecstatic about the babies. We're consumed by you. Olivier shows it better than I do, but he's also more deeply hurt by the emotional distance you've kept lately."

"I'm suffering from not knowing who you really are. I owe the Yore a greater debt than I owe you."

Gahariet stuck the fork in his cake.

"We're friends. We'll stand right by you when you announce the resurrection of your empire and make a claim for a reestablishment of a Yore nation."

His raised voice must have attracted Olivier, because Olivier, his eyes half open, drifted through the doorway.

He stood tall, though, as he said, "Our father stood by while he watched the Yore royals being destroyed. He didn't support it, but he didn't stop them, either. He knew that it would place him in jeopardy and set him against his own kind. But we are not our father. We are your mates, and we love you. We will love you until the end of eternity."

Phuong's eyes filled with tears at Olivier's declaration of love, given from the heart. Her heart was thumping in her ears.

She didn't know how to handle the overload of emotion, so she turned from the brothers.

But they instantly turned into smoke and circled her, pulling her into a three-person hug.

"We'll love you forever," Gahariet whispered into her ear before biting her earlobe and sending the beginning sparks of a bonfire through her body.

Olivier backed up from her and took a kitchen stool. He untied her dressing robe, letting it drop to the floor. The twins got naked, too.

"Put your stomach on the stool."

She looked down at it. It was cushioned. It shouldn't hurt the children. She still couldn't really see a baby bump.

She put her stomach down on the stool.

She could feel Gahariet's hands on her back, slowly massaging her as all the stress and tension left her body. She felt as relaxed as a cat in a sunbeam. Happiness spread throughout her body. They loved her. They would stand by her as she rebuilt the Yore people.

Then Gahariet's cock was guided inside of her, stretching her to her limits, making her moan. Olivier immediately took advantage of her open mouth to push his own erection inside of her mouth.

The two brothers pushed and pulled inside of her body over and over again until she lost track of time. They could have spent eternity there, lost in a haze of pleasure and love.

But finally it came to an end as both brothers exploded inside of her, making her feel complete.

"I love you," she declared.

## MATING CEREMONY

Phuong
## SEVERAL MONTHS LATER

*P*huong checked her hair in the mirror. She was getting ready to get ceremonially bound to the twin Thrones. She'd insisted on an oceanside ceremony.

Her ancestors would be able to attend in spirit. Literally.

Her dress was simple white silk that flowed over her large baby bump. She'd have her twins any day now. They had confirmed two heartbeats long ago.

At the beach ceremony, most of the guests were Draka. It looked like the wedding was overwhelming Draka. They couldn't see the Yore who were attending.

Phuong knew that neither the Yore or Draka were happy about the mating, but she didn't care too much. She hoped that their unease would fade over time. She knew that she would spend the rest of her life with her mates, building their empire together. They would put together the best possible kingdom for their children to inherit.

They hadn't arrived yet, but she knew that she already loved them with all of her heart. She wanted to raise the twice-royal twins the right way. She was facing a lot of political pressure from both the Yore and Draka, but the three of them would find a way.

"Are you ready?"

Xuan was going to walk her to her mate. They had no father. Xuan was her whole family for so long.

And now she was going to be ceremonially mated to the two Thrones. She put a hand on her stomach. She was going from having one family member to having five in one day.

"Ready."

She knew that if Xuan didn't approve of the Thrones, he wouldn't have agreed to walk her down the aisle. Xuan had gotten closer to the twins, but she'd tried as hard as she could in order to convince both sides to like each other.

She'd had to slow down her attempts at building a bridge between the Yore and Draka as her baby bump had grown, but she would declare her empire soon.

NEW EMPIRE

Phuong

She heard a baby's cry.

"A few more pushes," the healer coached. "Just keep pushing."

"I can't," she replied. "I don't have anything left."

"Whether you have anything left or not, your children are ready to be born. Your first one is already partially out. Your second one is coming fast."

"Ahh!" she screamed as her body shook in a powerful contraction.

They pulled the first baby out of her, the baby that came out of her womb crying.

"Keep pushing," the healer said.

"You're doing great, love," Olivier said. He was holding one of her hands while Gahariet was holding the other.

"I don't feel great," she said.

"Just one more and you can rest," Gahariet coaxed.

She screamed as she felt her muscles contract again. She was small, and Draka babies were quite big. They'd had to cut her to widen her in preparation for the delivery.

"That's it...another push!"

She couldn't stop her body from pushing out the second baby, who came into the world a little more quietly than his older brother.

Both of the babies were boys, just as Hoa had foretold. There were healers who were washing the babies and weighing them. The first baby had loud lungs. The second baby was a little quieter, but they spanked the baby, and it turned out that his lungs were just as good as his older brother's.

"It's time for the parade."

Phuong stared at Gahariet.

"What are you talking about?"

"In Draka culture, we parade our children as soon as they're born, so that our people know them."

"I'm a mess," Phuong protested. "I've been in labor forever."

"You don't have to look glamorous," Olivier said. "You're beautiful just the way you are. We just go out in an open levi-car."

Phuong closed her eyes. "You're going to have to carry me out."

"No problem."

In no time at all, the twins were wrapped in blankets. Phuong was presented with an over gown that went over her medical bay attire.

"You planned this."

"We knew you wouldn't want to be out so soon, but it's mandatory."

Phuong knew that she would've said no, but at the moment, she'd go along with whatever she needed to do in order to give the babies their rightful due as Draka and Yore royalty.

Olivier picked Phuong up while Gahariet and a healer carried the babies downstairs. Then they were getting into a levi-car, where Phuong lay back.

The streets were thronged with Yore and Draka alike. The cheers rang loudly, making Phuong's ears ring.

She smiled and waved at the people who were ecstatic about her children. These were her subjects...their subjects. It was a new dawn. Their love was destined to fix Vestra. One day, her children would be able to unite both races peacefully.

## OUTFOXING THE ALPHA

Carson Warner approached the corner of Pier and Avalon. He glanced at his watch, the classic Rolex read 1:55 pm. He looked back at the corner, no one was waiting.

*Damn.* He thought to himself, he had carefully timed his arrival to make sure he would approach Frankie at exactly 2. He wasn't going to be standing there waiting for him like a lonely puppy.

Carson Warner knew a thing or two about strategy. He couldn't be late, but he couldn't be the first one to arrive. He needed to send the message that his time was more important than Frankie's, that he was doing Frankie the favor by agreeing to meet him here.

Looks like Frankie knew a thing or two about strategy too.

Carson stopped a block away from the designated corner and watched. No one. Carson sighed deeply and calmed his anger. He turned toward the river front.

*His* river front. Almost his. If things went well with Frankie the Man, that would change. It would finally be all his.

When Carson Warner arrived in the city several years ago, he'd found the river front to be prime hunting territory. Over run with small timers -- mostly pigeons and rats. But then, what other animals had adapted so perfectly to city life among humans?

He had claimed the territory for himself and before long he had eliminated most of the worst elements. Word got out that the water front had a new apex predator and those that hadn't been done in by his hunting had scurried off to find new space.

Combined with the efforts by his fox, Carson's company soon began accumulating the property along the river. The city had kicked in millions of dollars to contribute to the restoration of the area. A new pedestrian path running along the west bank had enticed trendy restaurants and new hotels and shops.

The new marina was owned by Warner holdings and Carson approved of the luxury yachts slipped along the docks.

Even the east bank's industrial area had been spruced up, providing a pleasing view for the diners and shoppers across the river with newly refurbished loft condos set among the still operating docks with their cranes and shipping crates and the big ships coming and going daily.

Carson frowned at the big crane that was busy loading shipping containers onto a large ship.

East Shore Shipping.

It was the last piece of the puzzle. The last remaining piece of the waterfront that was not owned, at least in part, by Warner Holdings.

Carson glanced at the watch again, then back at the corner. He stopped a few hundred yards from his destination and decided to wait and see if Frankie showed up.

After 7 months of relentless requests for a meeting with the owner of The East Shore Shipping Company, Carson Warner was not about to miss his opportunity to present his offer to Frankie "the Man" Mansfield, even if the venue Frankie had insisted on was less than the ideal location for a business meeting to discuss a multi-million dollar deal.

1:59 pm. Carson's nerves twitched. From his vantage point, he could see a blonde approaching the corner. A tall, shapely woman in an expensive suit; white blazer, matching pencil skirt hemmed just above her knees, silk blouse, bright blue scarf worn neck-tie style, knotted loosely at the collar. An impossibly attractive woman that reminded Carson of a classic Hollywood femme fatale.

She was a beauty, that was sure but Carson was here on business, not pleasure. He watched the woman walk confidently across the street before he turned back toward the docks.

2:01 pm.

Carson was irritated. He'd been told to be on that corner at precisely 2 o'clock in the afternoon to meet with Frankie "The Man." Looked like he'd been played. He walked down the docks on the look out for the man he had come to meet. They were, after all, Frankie's docks. For the time being.

Carson walked among the towering stacks of shipping containers, paused briefly to watch the cranes working, before turning and walking back up toward the city streets.

As he passed a stack of wooden crates, he found himself face to face with the stoic blonde.

Up close he was able to take in her beauty in far greater detail, the pale perfect texture of her skin, the blue of her eyes set off by the scarf. Her hair was near platinum, no trace of dark roots near her scalp where her hair was pulled back from her forehead into a tight French twist.

The woman stepped out and stood purposefully before him. She was standing very close, invading his personal space and staring at him cooly with clear azure eyes lined with soft dusty blond lashes.

"You're late." The blonde's voice was ice.

Carson found himself at an unusual loss for words. No one ever challenged him like this. Certainly not women.

He inhaled her scent deeply-- easy at this close range-- she was human. No trace of animal about her. Making the confidence of her proximity even more confusing.

"I believe you were informed that you were to be on the corner of Pier and Avalon at precisely 2 pm." Her eye contact was deliberate... and unnerving. "It is now 2:04, Mr. Warner. This meeting is moot."

Carson was silent. He studied her intently as she spoke. Most females this close to him smelled of fear-- or arousal-- or a combination of both. This woman smelled of *power*. Strong, confident, unwavering. Her scent matched her demeanor perfectly. Power and...something else. Something Carson couldn't place. Something that curled around inside him, teasing at the corners of his consciousness, distracting him. Something that made him want to wrap the blonde woman tightly in his arms and kiss her hard.

She didn't wait for his reply. She turned and walked away. Carson watched her purposeful stride as she made her way to the white Bentley waiting across the street from the intended meeting spot, her long legs disappearing inside before her slender arm reached out to pull the door closed.

He'd been dismissed.

Carson Warner was not used to being dismissed. Carson Warner did the dismissing. He stood where she had left him, watching the car disappear into city traffic, leaving him to wrestle with the details of their encounter on his own.

Get the rest of the story now: Part 1